E

Publishing

Watch for More Titles
from Tamelia Keaton

and *Empower Publishing*

A Scared Life
To a Loving Wife

By

Tamelia Keaton

Empower Publishing
Winston-Salem

Empower

Publishing

Empower Publishing
302 Ricks Drive
Winston-Salem, NC 27103

The book is a work of fiction and is entirely the product of the author's creative imagination. No actual person, place or event is referred to in this work. The author has represented and warranted all ownership and/or legal right to publish all the materials in this book.

Copyright 2024 by Tamelia Keaton

All rights reserved, including the right of reproduction in whole or part in any format.

First Empower Publishing Books edition published
July, 2024
Empower Publishing, Feather Pen, and all production design are trademarks.

For information regarding bulk purchases of this book, digital purchase and special discounts, please contact the publisher at publish.empower.now@gmail.com

Cover design by Pan Morelli

Manufactured in the United States of America
ISBN 978-1-63066-604-0

Dedication

This book was written to bring awareness to stalking and to let everyone know that you should always stay aware of your surroundings. It is also to let you know that the weapon may form but it will not prosper and that no matter what your situation is God can still make it work out for your good.

—Tamelia Keaton

A Scared Life to a Loving Wife

1.
Day in the Neighborhood

It was a sunny day in the neighborhood where kids were playing kickball, skating and playing games like hide and seek, which were games kids loved to play before the streetlights came on. Everyone knew what would happen if you were not in the house before the streetlights came on. Adults were in the house doing their own thing and enjoying the break away from their children. The apartments were side-by-side, looking just alike, and in the back were sand barrels kids used to hide from other kids or just to get some shade when the sun was beaming on them.

That's what Layla enjoyed most, just relaxing in the barrel doing her own thing. Layla didn't like the heat much, so she would sit in the barrel and sing and do her own little thing. Layla was six years old. Her mother was a third shift nurse at the hospital who had three other daughters.

Layla's mother, Cindy, was always on the grind to support her daughters and possibly get her and her girls out of the Hood. Cindy had to do it alone because she knew she wouldn't get any help from her crackhead boyfriend. He slept during the day and chased the glass pipe by night. Layla and her sisters were very independent and knew how to take care of the household on their own. Layla had a ten-year-old sister named Diamond and a sixteen-year-old sister who made sure to hold their mother down at night by any means necessary. Layla loved to sing, read books and write poems and was the prettiest thing ever. She had a heart to always make people happy and never started any trouble with anybody.

The streetlights were beginning to dim and Layla noticed that she no longer heard the other children playing around her, meaning everyone had started heading home to make curfew and avoid punishment or the switch. Layla came out of her hiding place to head home when she was snatched by two boys that looked to be the size of men. As Layla screamed and kicked to try and get free, her tiny little body had no chance of preventing the men from taking her to where they wanted her to go. She was taken down some steps and into what seemed to be a boiler room or a maintenance room where the maintenance men should have only had the key. Why was this door not locked? The boys seemed to be in their 20's. One was brown-skinned, small framed, with an afro and short. The other was medium built, brown skin with a low haircut. Layla was trying to scream, but nobody heard her over the boiler room with the door being closed. Layla realized that she wasn't going to make curfew and her mother was going to be so mad that this was happening.

The floor was cold. There was no carpet. The room was dark and smelled like a gas stove. While the men took off Layla's clothes, including her panties, they held her down while they were also undoing their belt buckles. While one held Layla down the other entered her and pain shot through Layla's little body as she

A Scared Life to a Loving Wife

screamed and cried. One of the men started complaining about his time. The men switched roles and the other man enjoyed entering Layla as well. It seemed like eternity but Layla had already left her body and zoned out to her safe place where there was no more pain.

When Layla came back to reality the men were gone and Layla was left with the aftereffects which were blood running down her legs and filthy clothing soiled by the men's seeds. The only thing Layla thought about is how she was going to upset her mother because the streetlights were already on. Layla put on her clothes and at the speed of lightning ran out the door, up the steps and looked around to notice that she wasn't that far from home. When Layla got to the door, she stopped to make sure she was half descent and braced herself for the whooping. Surprisingly, her mother had not woke up for work yet and her stepfather was already on the scavenger hunt for his next high.

Layla ran and immediately jumped into the tub to wash off the scent and the memories of what just happened to her. She decided to not tell anybody because no one was going to believe a six year old little girl, and who were these men anyway. The stress got to be too much, so Layla cried herself to sleep.

Layla was asleep and was awakened by the sunlight beaming onto her little face. Immediately the aching between her legs and in her stomach was excruciating and the memories fled back. Bits and pieces of the men would come back into her mind making her cry all over again.

Her mom came into the room after coming home from work and Layla immediately put on a show. She stopped crying and made sure her mom had a good day at work. Layla asked her mom if she wanted some cereal and then her mom asked, "What time did you get in last night?"

Layla had never lied to her mom but found one fast. "I came in early, Mom. You were already sleeping.

Her mom answered, "I guess you are right. I was extremely tired last night. Let's eat our cereal so I can get a little sleep."

Layla jumped up to go to the kitchen and noticed the pain there again. After her grunt, Mom asked if she was okay and lie number two came out of her mouth. Layla said, "Yes."

After she finished her cereal with her mother, she told Layla to go clean up her room while she checked on the other girls. Cindy tells Layla that she could go out and play after all the chores. Layla had zoned out at the mention of outside but came back and said okay.

2.
THE HOOD GOES ON

The kids were out playing again and the hood was full of fun, but not for Layla. She was too sore to run and play. Those men had stolen her innocence and her little safe place to hide, which had been the sand barrels. Now she didn't want to sing or write poems. She just found herself sad, zoned out and wanting to commit suicide. She had to face every girl's worst nightmare at such a young age. Not only that, Layla found herself lying often to her mother to cover up the truth that she had lost her innocence to not one but two men that she didn't even know.

Layla was in her own little world when she heard her mother shouting her sisters and her name to come inside. She ran home and Mom said that they were going to the grocery store. Layla got dressed and jumped in the car with the old man that always drove them around because Cindy never had a driver license or drove a car before. The car was a blue old station wagon and the driver's name was Woodrow, who was old and creepy and seemed to always be friendly to the women and children. Layla always noticed that he would try to touch her or her sisters and tell them how pretty they were but Layla trusted her mom so he couldn't be that bad right?

Today was different, he kept looking at Layla in the mirror and giving her these weird looks and sounds which made her feel very uncomfortable which caused the other night to come back and how uncomfortable she felt now and then. After going to the store Cindy and the girls got back home, Layla talked to her mother about it and her mom said to go to her room because she was being extra dramatic, which caused Layla to really forget about talking to her mom about the other thing. Layla obeyed and went to her room and cried herself to sleep again.

3.
Go Away Bad Dreams

Layla woke up screaming and shouting and yelling, "STOP, STOP, HELP!!!"

Her sister Tonya came in and woke her up with a hug and telling her it would be okay. Sweat was pouring off of Layla's body and she noticed that she had also wet the bed. Layla was very embarrassed. Tonya and Layla were very close and Tonya always looked after her like a mother. She helped clean Layla up and put on some clean clothes. She ensured that she wouldn't tell Mom about the accident and that it was their secret. Layla was so proud because she didn't want to make her mother upset with her.

The nightmares continued every night and more and more details would come back. One day Layla even saw Woodrow in one of the dreams and woke up confused. It couldn't be him, could it? Layla knew that nobody would believe her so she swore to never tell anyone. Another day was here and Momma needed to get things for Sunday dinner, so she called Woodrow to take the girls to run errands. Layla got dressed, but was very tired from the lack of rest because of the nightmares, and the details were fresh on her mind.

Layla and her sisters were getting in the car when Layla froze when she saw that somebody was in the passenger side of the car with Mr. Woodrow today. Layla's heart was beating faster than a drum when she walked to get into the car and the passenger looked at her with a sinister grin. He was one of the guys who had taken her innocence. Why is he here? Who is he? More questions were coming when she heard her mother say Layla stop being rude and speak to Mr. Woodrow's son, Wilson. Layla could hear her heart coming out of her chest when she passed out.

Layla was awakened by hearing her mother and sisters yelling her name, asking if she was okay. Lights flashed in her eyes. She was not at home. She immediately knew she was at a doctor's office when she saw the lady in all white like her mom wears when she works at the hospital. The doctor said that all her tests were ok and maybe something scary caused her heart to beat too fast and she passed out.

Layla started to panic again when she wondered if the doctor had seen down there. Did her mother know? The diagnosis was a panic attack. Layla was relieved. Mom was looking sad and her sisters were in the waiting room, waiting to see her. Layla wanted to see Tonya and they said that it would be okay if her sisters visited her. Tonya rushed in and immediately embraced Layla with a motherly hug and at the moment she knew everything would be okay.

4.
Twelve Years Later... Miss Independent

 Layla walked in the neighborhood turning heads of both boys and men. Layla had matured into every boy or man's perfect girlfriend. She had long shoulder length hair and a caramel complexion with pretty hazel eyes. She had a slim figure with the complement of a flat stomach, thick in the waist and long pretty legs. She was your pretty tomboy who was competitive in all the sports including football. Layla and her sisters dominated the neighborhood in all games like video games, jump the creek, and kickball. The sisters were known not to take any junk and would deliver on a butt whooping if you messed with them. There was something about Layla that kept the neighborhood boys wondering why she wasn't involved in a relationship.
 At sixteen, Layla was a confident woman on the outside but a curious little girl on the inside, so she never gave in to the offers from the boys. Layla was a freshman at a majority black high school and was already hated by all the seniors because she was a dedicated athlete who came in and blew seniors out of their track spots. So, of course, the boys wanted to know all about the freshmen or "fresh meat" as they called it. The older boys even gave her a nickname,

"Lightning," because she was just that fast. She could give them a head start and come back to beat her competitors. Layla didn't understand why the girls hated her so much. She didn't act like she was all that and was very easy to get along with. Maybe that was why she was friends with the boys, because she understood them and wanted to play the same games they played. She was very competitive and smart. Not only was she a good athlete but she was also top ten in her class in academics. Colleges were already looking at her to see if she would be a good fit for their track team. Layla was serious about the sport. She practiced daily even on the weekends and she was not a stranger to the weight room. Rain didn't even stop her and she had male friends on the track team that would push her even harder to train with them which made her even better. She was a star and her main events were 100 meter, 200 meters, anchored 4 by 1 and 4 by 2 relay.

Layla wanted to have friends but she didn't entertain immaturity. She was independent and believed in getting it herself. She also worked a part time job at Food Lion. She saved her own money to purchase her own car and was helping her mother and sisters manage the household because of course her mother's boyfriend was still up to his old tricks and had gotten much worse. Layla and her sisters had to fight to keep each other safe. Not only was their mother's boyfriend trying to come into their room, but his crackhead friends thought that they could touch them or use them to get money to support their habits.

A Scared Life to a Loving Wife

Layla and her sisters were strong and would protect each other at all costs. Cindy and the boyfriend would fight on the regular and the girls would jump in and fight by any means necessary. They all had a plan to save as much as they could and find an escape route so that their mom wouldn't have to be with him anymore. They understood that their mother had to help people, pull those thirteen hours in the healthcare world and that their part was to hold down home and ensure the bills were paid. Layla's mom raised her girls to do better than her. So they would never have to depend on a man to pay their bills and to have their own. She also told them that they probably wouldn't meet a married man because they will be all single to get what they want. The girls would laugh but didn't really know what it meant at the time.

5.
Close Call

Layla needed to relieve some stress, so one Saturday evening she decided to get some practice in so decided to go to the track. Nobody was there so she started to stretch and take a couple laps around the track. While running an uneasy feeling came over her when she noticed a shadow in the woods just watching her. She knew it was an older man but she couldn't make out any features. It made her start wondering how long he had been watching her and if he had followed her there. She started to run around the track so she could try to get a closer look but when he noticed her, he disappeared into the trees which led to a trail to the recreation center beside the track.

Layla thought nothing of it because she knew she had to go into work tomorrow and wouldn't be able to work out. She got about an hour and a half with her steps, conditioning and her fast take off from the blocks and then decided to call it quits and go get some food and head home. Layla noticed a blue station wagon parked across the street with tenant windows with a man sitting in the car watching her, so she sprinted to her car, got in and looked in her mirror. She noticed that the station wagon wasn't there anymore. Could this have been the same man watching her?

Layla thought that she was being paranoid, so she went to get food and went home to call it a night. When

A Scared Life to a Loving Wife

Layla walked into the house, she was startled to hear her mother talking to someone over the phone about Woodrow passing. She was going on and on about how he was always there to take her on her errands and how his poor son would be all alone because his mother was dead and that she would attend his funeral. Layla had tried to move on past those events in the past but thought about it often. Her thoughts were interrupted by her mom knocking on the door to tell her that they were going to the funeral.

6.
The Funeral

Cindy, Layla and her sisters walked into the crowded church, waiting to be escorted to see the body. Layla dreaded even being there so she just tried to hide behind her mother so that she wouldn't have a panic attack. She had never been to a funeral but definitely wouldn't have chosen to come to this one. After viewing the body, Cindy walked over to greet the son and Layla hid behind her sister Tonya with no eye contact made to anyone. For some reason her confidence went back to when she was a youth who was scared to go play outside.

Wilson sat unmoved by the Pastor, speaking enhanced lies about his father being a good man. Wilson's mind wandered off on all the nights he was locked in the basement only getting bread and milk to eat while his dad invited strange streetwalkers in the house, making cat noises while his dad made howling sounds. Wilson had a lot of anger so when he could he would take his anger out by killing small animals since he was too afraid to confront this demonic man he had to call dad.

Wilson starts recalling the nights his dad would beat his mother like a boxer would his opponent. Afterwards, his dad would then rape her until his mother would pass out. One day his mother never came home and his dad made some excuse that she left him

A Scared Life to a Loving Wife
because she didn't love them. Wilson didn't believe it and it was confirmed when his mother was found in an alley, naked, raped, beaten and dead with a needle in her arm. They ruled it as a homicide but nobody was charged for it because they thought that she was a prostitute. Wilson knew that his dad had everything to do with it.

There was a window in the basement where he could see children playing and teenagers necking with each other. One day Wilson saw a pretty girl walking alone on the street and thought he saw her looking at him. Wilson was able to say hello through the window. When she heard this, she ran away and called him a freak.

Wilson had taken a long walk down memory lane and was interrupted by a beautiful woman and the most beautiful girl he had ever seen sending their prayers to him. Wilson noticed the girl stayed hidden behind her mother. Though she never did any of the talking, she must have been his angel. She had caused his thoughts to turn positive as he imagined them living happily ever after and raising a family. He had never felt this way about anything else. He felt an instant connection and knew he had to find out more about who she was. More people came to hug him but he could not think of anything or anybody else but her.

7.
The Stalking Begins

The day after the funeral, he found out that at least his mom and dad left him a paid off house and a lot of money in the bank. He still had his dad's paid-off station wagon, so he was doing pretty good. He landed a job as a maintenance man at a lucrative apartment complex where mostly college kids, single women and men lived. Wilson was even able to stay onsite for free so he could stay on call when he needed to.

Wilson bought a telescope and set it up in his apartment where he would work in the day and watch the women who stayed there at night. Wilson was very antisocial and afraid to approach a woman if he wanted. They always looked at him like he was weird. But what did he need them for? He already knew who his wife was supposed to be. So he would just please himself thinking about how good she was and how they would one day live happily ever after. This didn't stop Wilson from watching women in their apartments with his telescope, hoping that he would find the one person he loved most, the angel from the funeral.

One Saturday evening, Wilson wanted to get away from work, so he went to get ice cream from the store and parked by the high school to catch a breeze from the shaded trees. It was a nice day, so Wilson decided to get out of the car and eat his ice cream. As he was eating, he noticed a beautiful view of a girl working out

A Scared Life to a Loving Wife

on the track. He kept watching from behind the trees to get a closer look. Then he knew it was meant to be because it was the angel from the funeral. He watched how dedicated she was and he knew that she was an athlete because she was running with speed and was as beautiful as she was at the funeral. He became so fixated on her that he didn't even notice that she had caught him watching. It seemed that she was trying to get closer, so he went back to his car hoping that he didn't startle her. He was so in love that he didn't leave. A part of him wanted to get a closer look, smell or even a touch.

He noticed that there was one car and nobody was around. So it had to be her car. It was a blue Honda Accord clean and fit for her. Wilson was so curious that he waited in his car. He started to stroke his manhood thinking about his wife to be and that he would wait as long as he needed to see her again. After about an hour, she sprinted to her car. She seemed to look his way, so Wilson pulled off and left before she got suspicious. Wilson drove back to his apartment to finish what he started by thinking about her while stroking his manhood, imagining his seed in her while he relieved himself in a towel. He fell asleep thinking about her and how he wanted her all to himself at any means necessary.

8.
Eighteen and Still on The Grind

Layla walked into her job and it was already busy. Layla hit the floor running which included bagging groceries and helping run the office desk with refunds for customers. Layla was about to get on the register when her manager asked her to put some cold meats back so they wouldn't go bad.

As she walked down the condiment aisle, she spotted the cutest guy she had ever seen. He was six foot, brown skin with skin as smooth as silk. He was wearing a green collar shirt with blue jeans and matching green shoes. He had a gold earring in his left ear. Layla was so busy watching him that she didn't even notice that he was also checking her out. He seemed to also like what he was seeing, as he gave Layla an admiring eye from head to toe as their eyes finally met.

He politely spoke hello to her and Layla was all of a sudden mute. Words would not come out of her mouth. She finally got enough courage to speak, but immediately put her focus back on the task of putting away the meat and getting back up front to help on the register. Layla opened her register and noticed a car just sitting out front. Someone was in the car, but he never got out. Layla assumed he was waiting for someone to come out of the store. Her mind wandered to who was that fine piece of a man that God had

A Scared Life to a Loving Wife

perfectly made. Layla was afraid he would come through her line and she would again make a complete fool of herself again. What was wrong with her? She had always been so confident but it was something about him that made her feel not in control anymore.

That's when she noticed that he was standing at the end of her register and immediately she got nervous all over again. Sweat started to form in her hands and her body started itching and she began to fidget a little. She played it cool and when he was next in line Layla felt as if her face was red as an apple and that her heart was beating too fast to function correctly. He spoke with a deep baritone voice and Layla about lost it all together. He again spoke to her and asked, "Are you new around here because I wouldn't have forgotten a pretty face like yours?"

Layla smiled and informed him that she was only part-time because she was in school and an athlete.

He asked her what school she was at and asked her her age. Layla told him that she was 17 and would be 18 in a couple of weeks. He told her that he was 25 and in graduate school at Wake Forest University, studying to become a doctor. Layla was amazed and sad at the same time because she knew he would think that she was too young. He was so easy to talk to that she forgot she was even working. Layla had the biggest crush on him. He paid for his groceries and said that he would talk to her another time if that was okay.

As Layla watched him walk out the door, she noticed that the station wagon was still sitting there. The more she looked at it, the more familiar it became.

This was the same car that was parked watching her the night before during her workout. Layla began to panic. She didn't know what to do, but she knew this couldn't be a coincidence. However, as long as she stayed in the store with the police officer on duty she would be safe. She went on with her normal routine and thought that she would mention it to the cop and her manager once business slowed down.

Quitting time was coming and Layla was ready to go home. The crowd had slowed down and it was about 9 p.m. Layla looked outside and the car was gone, so she figured that maybe she had overreacted. Layla was about to clock out and decided to at least tell the police officer so he could at least watch her get into her car.

Layla walked to her car after looking around the parking lot and noticing the coast was all clear. Layla thought she would catch the BoJangles by her job to get something to eat before they closed at 10 p.m. before going home. She drove into the drive thru. As she was ordering her food, she noticed that a car that parked there turned its lights on and drove into the drive thru as well. Layla couldn't see the car too well, but she noticed it was a black male driving from the rearview mirror. He seemed to be paying close attention to her as she ordered. When she pulled to the window, she paid for her food and grabbed her food and left only to notice the car behind her did the same thing. He didn't seem to get any food. Therefore, this was very suspicious.

Layla got back on the main street to head home only to notice that she was being followed. Layla's heart

A Scared Life to a Loving Wife

started to beat a little faster as she tried to anticipate her next move. She got her phone out to let her mom know what was going on and at the same time took an alternative route to confirm her fear. Layla stopped using signals but made a right turn hoping to lose him, but the car did the same thing. Layla then made a sharp left then another right with a little more speed, but the car stayed on her tail. Layla felt panic rising when her mom told her to call the police and lead the car to the police station.

Layla did as she was instructed. When the 9-1-1 operator answered. Layla told the operator that she was being followed. They continued to ask her the routine questions and her location, her car model and whether she was able to see any details about the suspect. Layla told the operator that he was a black male and the car was a dark colored car. She told them that she was about to approach the police station and the operator said that an officer would be watching out for her. She looked in the mirror and the car took another turn and went straight when it seemed to notice that she was going to the police station. The police approached Layla and Layla was frantic and told the officer he was just there he must have gone straight. The officer said a unit would check it out and that she needed to do a report. Layla completed the report, mentioning the night before and the incident at her job as well and gave the police a better description of the vehicle. He added it all to the report and mentioned he would follow her home to ensure she was safe.

Layla called and let her mom know and she said that

she would be outside waiting for her. Layla finally got home and her mom and sisters were waiting on her. Layla said thank you to the police officer, grabbed her cold food out of the car. The police officer gave her a copy of the report and his business card and encouraged her to use it anytime she wanted to. Layla and her family went inside the house, and locked the door. Layla wasn't even hungry anymore; she just wanted to relax to calm her nerves down. She decided to take a bath instead to help her forget about the crazy day. Layla was relaxing in the bathtub when Mr. Sexy in the store flooded her mind. She closed her eyes and imagined if she would ever see him again.

Two weeks later...
    Layla woke up in the morning and decided to start her birthday weekend off with a good workout. She put on her workout clothes and got her motivational music in her ears. She drove to the track about to start her stretch when she received a conference call from her two best friends talking about the birthday plans for Friday night. They made plans to do dinner, and then go laser bowling, which was the hangout spot. There was good food, a DJ after a certain time and lots of people and lots of fun. Layla decided that would be fun and was already thinking about what she was going to wear.
    Layla finished her workout and that was when she noticed a man was watching her again from afar. Was this same guy watching her again from the recreation center? Layla immediately started to leave while calling the number from the card while walking to her

A Scared Life to a Loving Wife

car. She was almost to her car when she noticed a note on it. Layla's heart started to pound faster. She tried to calm down so that she wouldn't have a panic attack. She was informing the cop about the note and the cop told her not to touch the letter and to stay on the phone but to get in her car and lock the door and that an officer was enroute to meet her at her location.

From afar, she could see the car that was there last time she knew that she wasn't exaggerating. Layla continued to stay in her car but being observant with her surroundings and watching the mysterious car to see if she could see anyone. That's when she saw the police officer turning into her location which made her feel a lot safer. Then she saw the mystery man walking to the vacant car so she let the police know and the cop walked towards the car to confront the man.

While they were talking Layla wanted to call her mom to let her know. Her mom was upset and mentioned getting her some pepper spray to put on her key ring. Her mom was worried. Layla let her know that she would be fine but had to go because the cop and the person were walking back towards the car. Layla was so nervous to see the suspect but excited to know at the same time.

Once they got back to her car Layla looked at the man and something seemed very familiar about him. He was brown skinned, tall and nicely built and maybe in his early 30's. Something about him was creepy—or maybe it was the way he kept staring into Layla's eyes, like he was trying to see through to her soul. Layla was very uncomfortable. He seemed to be very educated by the way he spoke to the police officer. He apologized and told the cop that he didn't mean to startle her but he did community service everyday at the center to help keep it clean and couldn't help how beautiful she was and how athletic she was that he found himself watching but it wouldn't happen again. He admitted to putting the note on her window because she reminded him of this poem and wanted her to have it.

The officer asked if she wanted to tell him something and she told him that she wanted him to stop watching her and that she didn't think that it was cool and wasn't interested in him at all. The officer said he would do a report, but no charges could be placed because it was a public place. Layla was upset and felt justice wasn't served.

Then Layla remembered, what about him following me to the station is that a crime? Layla looked at the man and looked at the officer like he was confused. He told the officer that night he was at work and wasn't familiar with that incident. The officer shook his head in agreement with him and said that he would call him and get more information and he would do the same with her.

Just like that the officer waited until Layla got into the car safely and stayed around to talk with the man. Layla left feeling something wasn't right, but decided to investigate later. Now she had to get home to her family and get all of this out of her head.

After Layla left, the officer and Wilson talked like old friends and he thanked his friend for coming to his rescue so his cover wouldn't be blown. Wilson knew

A Scared Life to a Loving Wife

he was getting closer to having her all to himself. She was getting more beautiful everyday and he wouldn't let anything or nobody get in his way of his true love, not even his cop friend. Wilson knew that his friend felt the same way about Layla by the look on his face when he was talking about her, but Wilson believed his friend didn't deserve her. He had to get him out the way before he tried to make a move on her. So he needed a plan.

After Layla told her mom and sisters all the details, she was exhausted. She decided to go take a hot bath and a nap then wake up and start getting ready to hangout with her friends. She got excited and went to run her bath water. Layla was relaxing when Mr. Sexy flooded her thoughts and she was glad that she was now 18 so maybe she could get his number to have the opportunity to learn more about him.

Layla was having a good sleep when she was interrupted by a nightmare with the guy standing with the police. She was being raped by the cop and the guy, however her body was enjoying the feelings. Layla woke up to find herself wet between her legs, sweating and confused. Why was this feeling good and it should be a tragedy. Did the cop really know the guy?

Layla had too many questions and not enough answers. She thought it may be time to get some therapy and maybe that would help her heal so that she could be honest to her mother and could move on with her life. Layla had this fear of dating or even being with anyone because of the rape. Enough was enough but it wasn't going to happen on her birthday night!

9.
Party Time, He Turned Up

Layla was ready to enjoy her eighteenth birthday and couldn't wait to hang out with her friends. Layla decided to call her friends and see if they wanted to go shopping but was interrupted by a knock on the door. Layla looked out and saw her friends on the porch. She opened the door and saw balloons, bags, cake and other things. Layla was surprised and her friends had come to take her out to dinner. Layla was glad they had come by.

They talked while Layla looked through the bags and noticed they had her an outfit for tonight. Layla noticed that the outfit was the one she had in mind. High waist jeans with a bustier shirt that tied at the end and of course some nice heels to compliment the outfit. Layla knew what accessories she was going to wear with it. She was super excited now.

Layla had time to catch her friends up on the drama with the police station, the dreams and also Mr. Sexy from her job. The girls wanted all the details, and Layla also was telling them that she had received her acceptance letter for Wake Forest, St. Augustine, UNC Wilmington and Duke but was thinking about going to Wake to stay close. Layla's friends also said that they were going to Wake Forest and that they could all be roommates.

Layla got dressed so that they could go to dinner.

A Scared Life to a Loving Wife

Layla and her friends went out to eat at Texas Roadhouse which was one of Layla's favorite places to eat and decided to skip bowling and go to a little club called the In Zone. Layla always wanted to go but you had to be 18 to enter. Well tonight was the night.

The line was already long and by the glance of things there were already a lot of guys who were looking their way. Layla and her friends were something to look at. There was no ugly girl in that crew and all of them were smart and independent.

When they got in the club her friends paid for a VIP table so that they could have some privacy because the boys and men were already trying to separate them and make the girls their date for tonight. Layla was loving the vibe in this place and the DJ was on point.

She skimmed the club and noticed this guy in the corner watching her from head to toe. His face seemed familiar but she couldn't see him that clearly. Layla looked across the other side and noticed this tall, dark, fine specimen of a man from the back. Something leaped in her chest instantly. Layla thought maybe she could hit the dance floor with her friends. Layla and her friends were turning all heads when the fine specimen of the man turned around to see what the talk was about. Their eyes locked and it was love at first sight again at second sight.

It was him, Mr. Sexy from her job, and the man who was in her dreams and her fantasies. His eyes wandered all over her body while Layla continued to tease him with her hips swaying to the music. The song winding by R. Kelly was coming to an end, so Layla was starting to make her way back to her seat when he grabbed her hand. She turned around and their eyes locked.

He said, "Layla right?"

Layla was again embarrassed because she didn't even know his name. He read her mind and said, "My name is Mike."

Layla smiled and was lost in his eyes. She couldn't speak, she was confused as to why he could do this to her. She got very hot and said that she needed some water. He offered to buy the water when she heard her friends yelling for her to come back to the table. Mike saw the table with cake and balloons and realized that it was her 18th birthday. Mike brought the water to the table and asked the friends for permission to sit with their friend.

The girls immediately knew who he was because he was all Layla talked about. The girls agreed but then two other fine dudes came and said they were with Mike. It turned out to be a meet night with good clean fun. Layla and Mike were enjoying each other's company and so were the friends of both parties. Mike and Layla seemed to pick up just where they left off and talked again as if they had already known each other for decades. Mike and his friends all were studying to be doctors and Layla and her friends were all enrolling into Wake Forest to get degrees as well.

The DJ then played A Woman's Worth by Maxwell which was one of Layla's favorite songs and Mike asked Layla to the dance floor for a dance. Layla agreed and Mike took Layla's hand and led her to the floor to dance. They danced as if they were already in love and it seemed like the audience was watching as well. Most of the men and women were jealous, wanting spots because they were both the catch of the day and it ended up that they were each other's soulmates.

Wilson watched, enraged, from the back of the club. Layla and Mike danced like a married couple, which was why Wilson knew that this man was definitely keeping his wife in the blind from noticing him. He left in a hurry because he had to get a plan to remove him from her life.

The club was about to close and Mike wasn't ready for this night to end. This was like a dream come true. All he thought about after he had seen her two weeks ago was the hope they could meet in different circumstances, but he knew he loved her at first sight. She was the most beautiful girl he had ever seen and he knew that he needed her in his life forever.

The club closed and Mike and his friends walked Layla and her friends to the car. He held Layla's hand while he imagined her as his wife. Her pretty brown eyes and her goddess body was all he could think of. To top it off, she was smart, independent and athletic. He found out that they both ran track and both had a passion in the healthcare field. Mike had met his mate.

He said his goodbyes and asked for a date so they could continue their conversation and Layla agreed. They exchanged numbers and her friends did the same with their new friends and Mike told Layla to call him when she got home safely. Layla promised that she would. Mike told her that he wanted to get her a birthday present and Layla blushed. Mike was in love with everything about her, especially her smile. Her smile washed away anything that may have been negative and put joy deep down in his soul.

They went their separate ways and the girls talked nonstop about Mike and his friends. They all bragged on how they all were asked on dates.

This was definitely Layla's dream come true. Mr. Sexy was interested in her. She couldn't wait to see him again. Layla got home and called Mike and he answered on the first ring like he was waiting for her call.

He answered, "Hello, beautiful, you made it home?"

Layla was speechless but finally said yes. She thanked him for spending all his time with her at the club and for her birthday and that any place he picked would be fine for her for their next date because she wasn't choicy with food.

Mike was glad to hear that, but already wanted to give her the world. He asked to meet tomorrow evening because Mike said that he missed her already. Layla agreed and said that she had a long day and wanted to rest up for their date tomorrow. Mike said that he would pick her up around 2 p.m. Layla said that would be fine and gave him the address.

Layla went to bed and dreamed that she and Mike were on a beach and enjoying each other's company while Mike was rubbing his fingers through her hair. Layla's dream led to Mike and her about to make love

A Scared Life to a Loving Wife

when the guy from the club interrupted and hit Mike over the head with a bottle and yelled, "She is my girl, she is all mine!"

Layla went to comfort Mike when the guy grabbed her and she was being pulled farther and farther away from Mike. Layla woke up kicking and screaming Mike's name. When she woke up, Tonya was there protecting her and asking if she was okay. She was telling her sister about how much fun she had with her friends and how she met the guy from 2 weeks ago at the club and how she was excited to get to know more about him.

Tonya told Layla to be careful and to take things slow to make sure he is who he said he is. Layla promised and told Tonya that she was going to meet him tomorrow when he picked her up. Tonya said that she would make sure she got his tag number and location of where they would be just in case. Tonya let Layla know that she needed to start making a move because the time was getting late. It was 12 p.m. already and Layla didn't even know what she was going to wear.

He didn't give her an idea of where they were going, so Layla's mom suggested a black dress with heels. Layla took her mom's suggestion and was telling her mother how much she really liked him. He was older than she was but he was in Med school and attending Wake Forest as well. Her mother knew that she could handle herself so wasn't shocked that the guy was 25.

Layla's mom helped with her hair, so by 1:45 p.m. Layla was drop dead gorgeous and ready to go. The dress she went with wasn't too short or too long but knee length. She let her hair flow down her back with the curls her mother put in it and put on a nice pair of heels to give her class. The jewelry matched the heels very well. Layla didn't wear makeup, so she did her lips and was ready to go.

Layla heard the doorbell ring and noticed he was there already on time, which was a check in Layla's book. Nobody wants to date someone who comes late and think you are supposed to wait! Her mom and Tonya went to the door to meet the mystery man and let him in. Mike complemented his mother and her sister and told them that he can see where the girls got their looks from.

Mike was dressed in a black three-piece, black linen suit with some Stacey Adams shoes to set his outfit off. He was such a gentleman. Mike hit it off with her mother and Tonya which was what Layla needed to see to be confident. Her mother gave Layla the nod like she approves and so did Tonya. It was like Mike was already a part of the family.

Layla walked down the hall causing Mike to glance in that direction and his heart dropped on how much more beautiful she was today. It didn't help that he thought about her all night but seeing her again he saw a new beauty in her. She was a natural beauty. Mike reached for her hand and kissed it and asked was she ready to go. Layla said yes and both said their goodbyes to the family and walked outside. Layla was immediately amazed when he walked towards the black BMW seven series. There was a driver in the car.

A Scared Life to a Loving Wife

Mike opened the door for her and put her seatbelt on for her. He was such a gentleman and Layla knew why she wanted to date an older man. Layla had never got this type of attention and that is why she chose not to settle for just anyone because she could. Layla couldn't help but to stare at him in awe. She felt like a queen sitting next to a king. He got in the back with her, buckled his seatbelt and said that their appointment reservation was at 2:30 p.m.

Layla and Mike pulled up to an all-inclusive day spa, which Mike said was part of her birthday present. Layla got a manicure, pedicure and a full body massage. Everyone there catered just to her like she was a celebrity. Mike also got a pedicure, manicure and massage and seemed to know the owners pretty well.

After all the spoiling he said dinner was at 5 p.m. They pulled up to Ruth's Chris Steakhouse. Layla already knew that it was expensive because she and her friends talked about how one day after they get doctor status they would be able to afford it. The food was nothing but amazing. The steak was the best she ever tasted and the bill was well over $200, which didn't seem like a problem at all to Mike.

Mike wanted to spoil her more, but thought it would be wise to ease her into it. Mike knew he came from money so he was used to the finer things. He loved the fact that Layla wasn't looking for money like the other women were and Layla didn't know who he really was which made it better. He felt natural with her, like he didn't have to be on alert with women who just wanted the fame.

Mike was the only son of the most well-known neurosurgeon in the world. His dad was owner of two major hospitals which caused him to be on TV, in newspapers and he had even written ten books that hospitals use to help with patients.

Mike's mother was also very successful. She had a MBA and owned over fifty businesses and was also on TV, helping others start their own businesses and showing others how to invest money. Together they were worth billions with three to four mansions in different states, but they chose to reside in New York.

Mike, on the other hand, chose to stay out of the spotlight, so he joined the Army for four years, and decided to go to college to get his doctor's degree like his father. Mike enjoyed helping people.

Layla was relaxed and ready to spend more time with him. He said good because it was one more place he wanted to take her. By this time, Layla was ready to go to the moon with him if he asked her to. They ended up on the campus of Wake Forest, where excitement leaped in her stomach. This would be the school she would attend soon. There was a Starbucks café, which had a lounge full of students and teachers. Layla looked around and noticed everyone had the same book and there were more.

Mike held her hand while everyone stood as if he was a celebrity or something. There were cameras and several news crews on site as well. Layla was so nervous and glad that she picked the right outfit for the occasion. Layla smiled for the camera and continued to stand by his side. Mike sat Layla in the chair beside him and gave her one of the books.

Layla realized that they were at his book signing and that's when it happened. Mike started to quote one of his love poems to her which was named "Pretty Brown Eyes." Had he been writing about her? Mike was so amazing with his poetry. He was everything she dreamed of. She noticed how all the women wanted to be her or the lady he was writing about in the poem which made her nervous all over again. What if she wasn't enough for him? Was she ready for a popular man like this? Again she had questions with no answers.

The news reporters started asking questions about his parents and their next project and his success at Wake Forest and when was the next book coming out? That is when Layla knew that Mike was not just an ordinary guy. He was a millionaire and the son of billionaires. She was so lost in her own thoughts until she saw Mike looking at her and answering the question about who she was and how pretty she was and that they make a cute couple.

Layla didn't know what to do. She felt her face turning red and realized that she was very camera shy. The interview was finally over. Mike signed some books, sold others and just like that they were leaving.

When they got back into the car Layla started asking some questions. Mike was open and honest with her and let her know that he was popular because of his parents and now his book and that she would meet them very soon.

It was getting late, so he told Layla to call and check

in with her family. Her mom and sisters told Layla that they were on the news and how pretty she looked. Her mom also knew about his parents and their work and that she was a big fan and that Mike was everything he said he was.

Mike then asked her mother if Layla could stay the night at his place because it was late and his house was closer. Layla was shocked and at a loss for words. Her mom told Mike to take care of her baby. Mike gave her mom his address and phone number just in case she needed to call him.

They rode through a neighborhood where every house on the street was at least a million dollars or more. Layla only dreamed of living in houses like these. Layla was enjoying the view when they pulled up to a gate. Mike put in a code and the driver drove on to the long driveway. The gate closed and that's when she saw two men approaching the car. They were his personal security team who waited for their orders. Layla couldn't help but to look at Mike and how he can look so regular but be so important.

The garage opened and they pulled into where there were three more luxury cars. One was a Diablo, which was a Lamborghini. The car stopped and Layla sat frozen not knowing whether she was dreaming or if this was really real. Mike got out of the car and came around to open the door for her. He undid her seatbelt and grabbed her hand leading the way.

The house was immaculate. The house had everything you could imagine. It had eight bedrooms furnished with bathrooms to die for. It had two full

A Scared Life to a Loving Wife

kitchens, a dining room, a library and an office. It had an outside pool house with a heated jacuzzi.

There was a lady in the house cleaning who asked Layla if she could get her anything to eat or drink. Layla declined because she was still in this dream. Layla was told to make herself at home and that she could pick from any of the four guestrooms. She was about to get comfortable but then noticed that she didn't have any clothes. Mike told Layla that, when she agreed on the second date, he had his maid to go out and buy different clothes along with everything a young lady might need if she didn't have clothes. He wanted the closet to be filled with not only clothes but shoes, so she could see how the maid did. All the clothes and shoes were still in boxes and had the tags on them because what she couldn't wear they could take back and try again.

Layla knew this was a dream and her mouth was wide open. Mike made her dream reality when he took her into his arms in a bear hug. Layla hugged him back and told him that he was really spoiling her and that she never had any real dates. She explored the rooms and noticed one with a walk-in closet and a king-sized bed. She sat down in the chair in the closet to see what would be comfortable to sleep in and noticed that Mike had found his way behind her. He turned her around and stared deeply in her eyes. Layla embraced him and didn't ever want to let him go.

Layla had truly fallen in love with Mike. Layla had been waiting and it happened. They kissed and she had never felt her stomach do that before. The kiss was very sensual and then she felt it. She was turning him on and something hard started to invade her space. Layla looked down and noticed how big the bulge was in his pants and she backed away and broke the mood. Layla was flooded with fear because she had never done this before and she promised her sister that she would take it slow. Mike immediately realized that there was a change in the mood and apologized because he was so attracted to her that he couldn't control his body language.

She asked for some privacy and that she would like to talk about it. Mike gave her some space so she could get more comfortable. He told her to come down to the living room when she was ready. Layla decided to take a shower and change to a short pajama set from Victoria's Secret. His maid really had good taste and the bath gels smelled wonderful. She also decided on a house coat and some socks.

When Layla came out, she heard a song being played on the piano. She followed the sound of the piano and was amazed to see Mike playing like a pro. She didn't want to interrupt him so she just stood in the doorway and watched. Mike could feel her sweet presence in the room so he invited her over. Layla came and sat and started to play the keys for fun. Mike said he had been playing for years and had even won a piano award and even played for a couple of his parents' rich friends before.

Mike took her to the couch and said that she could talk to him about anything because he wanted to know who this woman was that held his heart. Layla

A Scared Life to a Loving Wife

hesitated at first but then started to tell Mike about the rape, the nightmares and how she was a virgin and had a fear of being with any man sexually. This surprised Layla because she never told anyone about it. However, getting it out made her feel a little better. Layla cried and shared what she had never even told her mother or sisters.

After it was all over Mike hugged her and told her that it didn't change the way he felt about her, that she was beautiful inside and out and that it wasn't her fault. He also said that he would never allow her to be hurt by anyone again. Mike shared all about his life and how hard it was growing up in the spotlight and trying to be who his parents wanted him to be. He said that he even had to date girls who were well off like him and wanted the money.

Mike told Layla that she should never feel pressured to do anything and that he would wait until she was ready but he wanted her to know something. Layla braced herself for the worst and asked him what it was. Mike admitted to Layla that when he saw her in the grocery store he was already in love with her and it inspired him to write poetry about her. Layla blushed and then admitted that she thought about him every night and wanted to be with him as well. Mike said that he wanted to take it slow but was very selfish and wanted her all to himself.

Layla blushed and hugged him and laid her head on his chest. Mike played with her pretty hair while planting soft kisses on her forehead. Before you knew it, Layla had dozed off to sleep in his arms. Layla got some of the best sleep she ever had without the nightmares. It felt so right.

Mike carried Layla to the bedroom she chose, laid his angel down, covered her up and watched her sleep. Her face was perfect. He prayed for her while she was asleep and then went off to his room down the hall and slept like the prince that he was. He knew that he would call his parents tomorrow because very soon he wanted to take his angel on a trip.

10.
I Want All of You

Layla woke up to sunlight and noticed that she was in the bedroom that she had chosen. Layla went to the door and started to explore the house a little bit more. She started checking out the other bedrooms and noticed one door was closed. Layla knocked but nobody answered, so she went in anyway. Layla opened the door and noticed the bed was empty but the shower was going. She was tempted to speak but decided against it.

Layla went downstairs to start breakfast because she was starving and wanted to get familiar with the kitchen. As she looked in the refrigerator she noticed some bacon, eggs and some bread. She found where the pans were and started to cook.

She didn't notice Mike watching her at the door. Mike was amazed that she could cook so well. He wasn't used to another woman cooking in the kitchen because he had gotten used to the maid cooking or going out to eat, but it was truly nice having this beautiful woman familiarizing herself with his kitchen. He could definitely get used to it.

Layla was done in a flash and turned around to notice Mike holding her from behind. She felt his bare chest and the feeling in her stomach invaded her again. How does he do this to her? Layla felt wetness between her legs and again she felt his strong manhood on her behind.

She put the food on the table and looked in the refrigerator for something to drink. Mike watched as Layla bent over to get some apple juice and his manhood started to jump again. Mike was confused as well on why he couldn't control his arousals when being around her. It was never like this with the other girls. His mind and body wanted to take care of her financially and he didn't want to rush her.

They ate breakfast and talked about college. Mike then told Layla that he wanted to talk to her mom when she got off of work. Layla said that would be fine. Mike then told her that he would like to take her out of the state for a while. Layla proceeded to tell him that she could not go and had to work. Layla explained to him that she was saving for another car and with expenses for her college tuition at Wake Forest. Mike was already selfish with her and wanted to support her financially.

After breakfast, they got dressed to go to Layla's house. Layla got home and her mom was in the kitchen crying. Mike walked in and noticed the change in the mood. Layla was comforting her mother because she said that her boyfriend had gotten hold of her bank card and spent all the bill money on drugs. She didn't know what to do.

Mike was very sympathetic and sad that her family had to endure this type of stress. Mike was about to speak when he heard a man cursing and screaming at her mother coming down the hallway. Layla's sister Tonya and he were in a heated argument and were about to fight. Layla left her mother to go to her sister's rescue and was about to jump in to help.

Mike watched and then stepped in to try to bring some peace. The security guard must have heard, because he moved Mike out of the way and took the man down in a flash. Mike was trying to get the man to calm down and told him that he needed some help.

Mike made a phone call to his father and told him about the man needing rehab. Mike's parents had connections everywhere and were able to set up some help for him free of charge. Mike left a card for the man and told him that if he was really serious about help he should call this number. In the meantime, Mike had to take care of his future family and get them out of this bind.

Mike and the security guard got back into the car with Layla and her family and brought them back to his home. Mike let them know that they could stay there as long as they wanted to. Security would keep them safe and they could choose any of the spare rooms upstairs and to make themselves at home. Layla's mother cried and thanked him for taking care of all of them.

Layla was upstairs with her sisters while her mother sat in the kitchen asking the maid for coffee. Mike then asks Layla's mom if she would be okay if he dates her daughter exclusively and could he take her daughter to meet his parents when they get back to New York. Layla's mom said of course and thanked him for being so respectful because she was eighteen and could make her own decisions.

Layla got her sisters to finally rest and she went

back down to be with her mother. Her mom smiled and reached for Layla's hand. Her mom told her that she was proud of her and that she was going to be an excellent student at Wake. Layla was happy that she made her mother proud.

Mike knew that he couldn't be without her.

A Scared Life to a Loving Wife

11.
Who's The Boss...

He came back into the kitchen where they were talking and her mom smiled. Mike asked Layla to come out of town with him and she said okay. He told her that they needed to run some errands first to ensure that her family had what they needed until they returned. Mike grabbed her hand and went to the car. When they got into the car and he buckled them both up he asked Layla if she would be his girlfriend. He told her that they could still take things slow, but he didn't want to share her with anyone else. Layla laughed and said that she didn't want or need anyone else.

He said that he was taking her to meet his parents because they had already heard so much about her and seen her on the news and can't wait to see her in person. Layla got nervous. Was she good enough to meet his parents?

Layla had to stop by her job and immediately everyone knew about Mike and his parents. Her coworkers treated her like she was a celebrity. They said that they saw them on the news and already knew about Mike and his parents.

Layla was there to tell her manager that she was going to take some time off when Mike told her boss that she may not be coming back to work. Her manager told Layla that she knew it already. Her boss said that the owner of the store called and found out that their son was dating their employee and she needed to be replaced. Mike's mother was one of the owners of the food store and had plenty of stock in the company. Layla was surprised.

Layla and Mike were shopping in the store when she noticed the blue station wagon parked outside again watching her with Mike. Mike noticed the man watching them as well, so he immediately let the security officer, who was already on it, know and told him to find out who he was. Mike got his PI on the case so he could see what he was all about. He was ready to defend Layla with his own life because that's how much he loved her already. When they left the store, the car wasn't there anymore so he made a mental note to ask Layla if she had recognized it as well.

They had all kinds of food and snacks so that her mother and sisters would be able to eat what they wanted to. Mike paid the bill which was very expensive but not a problem at all for him. Mike wanted to rest before getting on the plane and his love had never been on a plane, so all of this would be new for her. His secretary booked a flight for 8 p.m., leaving plenty of time to get some rest.

Layla and Mike arrived back at the estate with the security team. Layla figured that packing should be next on the list. She was all packed and spending time with her family when the alarm went off at the gate. Mike came down the stairs and told Layla and her family to follow him to the safe room at the bottom of the house until the security team told him that all was

A Scared Life to a Loving Wife

okay. Layla immediately started to panic, but when going into the safe house she realized that nothing or nobody could get in to get them. Everything you needed for a storm or if you were stranded you would be okay for a while. Layla thought how smart he was to think about this but then remembered that he may have had a lot of things happen like this because of who his parents were and because he was rich. The security team said that someone had tried to get in the gate and they believe it could have been the same man from the grocery store.

Panic set in the pit of Layla's stomach when she remembered that she didn't tell Mike about the incidents with the stalker. She told him everything. He then told her that she had nothing to worry about and that she and her family now could be targets and that they all will be safe with him and his team. He told his PI everything and said he needed to get someone trailing them constantly due to the circumstances.

Mike was hanging out with the PI when his lead detective knocked on the safe room's door. Mike let him in and a security guard showed him the news clipping where a cop and a young girl's body was found. The news clipping revealed that they were still looking for the suspect, but the car was similar to the car that was on the camera and the store but couldn't confirm the license plate number.

Mike was in deep thought, trying to connect the dots. He was thinking that maybe the trip was much needed for everyone just in case this was the same dude who was stalking his future wife. He knew that Layla would be worried about her mom and her sisters, so he made some phone calls to arrange his secretary to work on changing the tickets and also getting tickets for her family to come to New York as well. He called a family meeting to ensure everyone was on the same page about how serious this could be. He said that, in order to guarantee everyone's safety, everyone must follow the orders from his security team. Everyone was on board.

Layla was talking to her mother and sisters about everyday situations, but Mike then made them aware of what the news was saying not finding the suspect. Mike wanted to ensure he had every detail about Layla's incidents so he could give them to his security team.

Mike asked Layla's mother if they could all go out of town with them. She said that she had to go to work, however she had accumulated a lot of paid time off and thought, with everything happening, going out of town didn't sound bad at all. She said she would let him know after she talked with her boss. Mike made a mental note to make some phone calls on her mother's behalf.

Mike looked at Layla and noticed joy and relief on her face and thought about how he wanted to make her happy like that for the rest of his life. He told them that Layla and he would be flying out at 1 p.m. tomorrow instead of that night and for her mother to let him know ASAP what she decides to do.

It was getting a little later and everyone wanted to start winding down because they all had a big day

A Scared Life to a Loving Wife

tomorrow. He thought it would be best to order pizza for dinner instead of getting his maid to cook this late, so she ordered the pizza. After everyone ate, they all retired to their own areas of the house to start packing or resting, however, Layla and Mike ended up in the living room area by the piano. Layla started playing the keys and Mike listened, enjoying every minute with her. The thoughts that Mike was having right now about her were out of this world. How could she make him feel like this and they hadn't even explored each other in that sexual way yet? He knew he had definitely met his soulmate. He knew she was young and he didn't want to rush her, but he knew that he needed her for the rest of his life and hoped that she felt the same way.

    Layla noticed that Mike was in deep thought and she felt a shift in the mood. Layla walked to Mike and started to massage his shoulders and said that she wanted a penny for his thoughts. Mike came back to reality and told Layla that he was madly in love with her and that he never felt this way before and that he was struggling to control his sexual desires around her. Layla was amazed that someone felt that about her, though she was nervous that she wasn't enough for him and his lifestyle. Mike intercepted her thoughts and told her that she was all he needed, wanted and desired. He didn't want to go another day without her.

    Layla stood up and Mike grabbed her arm and gave her a passionate, heartfelt embrace. He looked down into her beautiful hazel eyes and their tongues locked for it seemed like eternity. The feeling immediately returned to her stomach. She decided not to fight against it. She gave in to the mood to see how far he was going to take it.

They kissed and he grabbed her and carried her to his bedroom. Her moans were turning him on passionately, causing him to become amazingly aroused. He ran his hands through her long, silky hair. Mike laid her on the bed, where he realized she looked like an angel. He planted soft kisses on her exposed belly, imagining that one day she would carry his seed.

Layla closed her eyes, overwhelmed by the pleasure of his gentle kisses. Mike laid beside her. For the first time, she began to have a strange feeling of arousal throughout her body. She gazed up at Mike with surprise and desire. Their eyes met with a mutual yearning, but also an awareness of her intention to remain chaste, and to refrain from giving in to the passion building within her.

Gently, Mike laid beside her, their eyes speaking their shared love and longing for one another. Layla knew this was a man she could trust with her body, her life and her love. Mike knew this was the true love of his life. As much as he longed to be one with her, he would wait until she was ready. They held one another in silent serenity.

Layla drifted off to sleep while Mike watched her and held her closely in his arms. When she woke up in the morning he would be right here with her just in case she had any feelings about what they just accomplished together.

Mike would make sure they accomplished every-

A Scared Life to a Loving Wife

thing together. Mike called his lead detective, Jon, to ensure everything was locked down and that the security team was in place. He then watched his angel a little more and went off to sleep dreaming that Layla was walking down the aisle to become his bride.

12.
Grown Woman Status

Layla woke up a new girl. All she could think about is how much she enjoyed the first night with Mike. The feeling in her stomach was as feeling she never experienced before. Did this mean that she wasn't a virgin anymore? She took a mental note to ask her friends and family for their opinions.

Layla still had some loose ends to tie up before their trip, so she figured to go downstairs and start breakfast for everyone. She went to the bathroom to freshen up and was headed downstairs when she smelled bacon already cooking. She walked in the kitchen to find Mike and her mom cooking and in a deep conversation about her. They noticed she was in their presence and both changed the subject.

Mike said, "Good morning, my queen."

Layla's mother had an angelic smile as if she was very happy for them. Layla spoke to both and went over to kiss her mom on the cheek. Mike just admired this beautiful picture and noted that Layla definitely had gotten her looks from her mother.

She hugged Mike, kissed him on the lips and immediately the feelings from last night came back. Layla stepped back and was embarrassed that she felt that way in her mother's presence. Layla needed to talk with her sister so she could shed a little light on the situation.

A Scared Life to a Loving Wife

Mike reminded Layla that the plane left at 1 p.m., so they should be leaving about 11:45 a.m. to give themselves plenty of time.

Layla went to the room where her sister was, knocked and went in. Her sister was packing and on the phone in a deep conversation, so Layla left and reminded herself to talk about it later.

Layla walked back up to the room and watched Mike at the table. He was sexy and the perfect gentleman. The maid came in and set up a table in the breakfast room and brought their food to the table. She asked if he would need anything else and Mike asked her to make sure they were not disturbed in the private breakfast room. Layla was nervous and excited at the same time to know that this man could give orders and be so gentle at the same time.

Mike took Layla's hands and led her to her spot by the table and then he sat beside her. He then looked into her eyes, cleared her pretty long hair from her face and gave her a serious look. Layla asked if there was something wrong and Mike said, "Nothing is wrong. Everything is right."

Layla blushed and Mike couldn't contain his emotions. Why did she make him feel like he wasn't in control? Layla ate a little and Mike asked her what her feelings were from last night. Layla blushed again and put her head down. Mike lifted her chin up so he could stare into her pretty hazel eyes that couldn't deceive. Layla let him know that it was the best feeling that she ever felt, however she wanted to wait until marriage to go any further. Mike understood and offered his apology for not being able to control his emotions. He mentioned how he wanted her all to himself and that he had fallen in love with her.

Layla was so happy he felt the same way and also admitted that being able to satisfy him scared her a little and that she worried she wouldn't be enough for him. He reassured her that he didn't want anybody but her and that he would never hurt her. He kissed her lips and fed her some bacon and toast.

Mike ate a little bit and told her that he couldn't wait until she met his parents. Layla was very nervous to meet his parents and hoped that they would like her. They finished eating, then Mike had the maid clean up. Layla remembered that she needed some last-minute traveling items and let Mike know that she had to go to the Walmart to pick up some personal things. She was going to take her sister, so that they could talk.

Layla got dressed and Mike grabbed some car keys and told her to take one of his cars, then asked if she wanted a driver. Layla decided that she wanted to drive the nice car. He told her he wanted her to take a security guard, but Layla insisted that she would be okay. He told her to be careful and to watch her surroundings. Layla promised and jumped in the Jaguar. Layla and her sister headed to Walmart. Layla could get used to this lifestyle but didn't want to get too comfortable yet.

Layla and Tonya talked about everything and Layla felt better knowing that she was still a virgin in spite of the sexual feelings she felt the night before. Layla pulled up to Walmart, parked and walked into the store.

A Scared Life to a Loving Wife

Layla and Tonya were both very pretty so everywhere they went boys and men were looking because they were gorgeous. They were in deep conversation when two men stopped them and tried to take them out and give them their phone numbers. Layla and Tonya declined and kept their conversation going, catching up on old times.

Wilson was walking around Walmart, trying to watch his next victim while getting more supplies to catch his prey, when he saw her. She was the prettiest creation that God had made and, as a bonus, she was with another beautiful girl who resembled her. They had to be sisters. Wilson thought how innocent and naive they were, because he had been following them for the last five aisles and they didn't even notice him. Wilson walked down the same aisles to smell her essence. They both smelled so good he had to find a way to get into their conversation.

While they talked, walked and shopped, Wilson listened and followed. Another two aisles later, Wilson noticed two other guys approaching the girls and immediately got jealous. The girls seemed to decline the offers. She had the prettiest smile and he felt he had to keep following her to protect her.

The girls went to the lingerie section and Wilson immediately got excited. He could imagine what she would look like in the nude and would give anything to be with her sexually. Wilson was in deep thought, so that he didn't notice that the girls had caught him in his own dark thoughts and moaning out loud. She yelled at him and called him a pervert and left to pay for their things. He saw the girls talking to the manager so he had to make a run for it before the police came.

As he ran out the door, the girls were pointing his way and were able to see his car. Layla froze when she realized this was the same guy who followed her home and was watching her run on the track. Why was he following her? Was he the one at Mike's house? Layla was frozen in place when her sister said that she had called Mike and that the police should be here soon. Layla felt hot, panic set in. Before she knew it, Layla had fainted and fallen to the ground.

Layla woke up and found herself in the back of an ambulance getting checked out. Her mom, sisters, Mike and the manager were talking to the police. Mike saw Layla awake and immediately came to her side. Police followed suit and, before she knew it, everyone was asking her questions, including the paramedics. Most of the questions were about her health but the others were about the strange man. The feeling came back and Layla could feel her heartbeat beginning to race again, alarming the monitor and the paramedics. They told her to stay calm and that she seemed to be suffering from panic attacks.

Mike grabbed her hand and the fear went away. What was it about this man that made her always feel safe? Layla's mom was supporting Tonya but stepped over to kiss Layla and assure her that she was going to be okay. The paramedics asked Layla if she wanted to go to the emergency room and Layla declined. Layla needed to get out of this state for a while, so she asked if Mike could take her home so she could finish packing.

A Scared Life to a Loving Wife

Mike gave demands to his driver and security guy and instructed Layla's sister to drive the car home with everyone, saying that someone would be following them back to the house for safety. Mike put Layla in his car with the driver and Layla laid back in the car to nurse her slight headache from all the drama. She decided to take some medicine when she got back to the house. Mike rubbed his fingers through her hair and held her as if he never wanted to let her go. Layla could lay in his sexy arms forever, however forever ended too fast when Layla felt the car come to a stop and the driver opening the door. Mike carried Layla into the house and took her upstairs. He laid her on the bed and ran her a bubble bath so she could relax.

He called his maid to get her some clothes and he undressed her. He admired her beauty and the image made him imagine her pregnant with his child. He had to get himself together. He had never thought about having children until now. She had to be predestined to be his wife and Mike couldn't wait to take that step.

Layla was relaxing in the tub when Mike startled her by getting into the bath with her. Layla laid her head back on his chest while he drizzled water on her breast and her stomach. Layla was so relaxed that she had forgotten about the hard day she just had in the store. Layla's hair was resting on his chest and getting wet at the same time.

Mike was loving the view of how beautiful her body was and again he couldn't control his thoughts. Mike's body started to react, forcing Layla out of her comfy spot.

Immediately the guilt came back as she wondered whether or not she was still a virgin. Layla knew things were starting to heat up and the thoughts of wanting to go all the way put fear in her heart. Could she please Mike; what if it hurts too bad; or, bigger problem, what if she got pregnant and all her dreams of college and running track would be lost? She didn't want that to happen so thought she would talk with Mike tomorrow.

On the other hand, Mike's mind was wondering, "What is she doing to me, why do I love her so much and how soon could she become my wife?"

The shower was very relaxing but packing had to happen. Layla and Mike kissed and went into their separate directions so they could both pack, because Mike had some plans for her. Layla was going to meet his parents.

Layla was looking forward to getting out of the state because there had been a lot going on lately and it was beginning to be too much. She was glad that Mike had come into her life and helped not just her but her entire family.

13.
Putting The Surprise Into Action

Mike had a lot of work to do. He had his assistant working to find Layla's mom and sisters a later flight to New York, as well as a place to stay on their own and maybe even a transfer for her job so that she could continue to help people but would also be safe. He knew his parents would love her.

Mike felt lonely even though he knew Layla was in the guest room down the hall. He missed her already and the thought of becoming one with her tantalized his mind again. She was nothing but amazing and he didn't know how he had gone so long without her in his life.

Mike finished packing and noticed he heard talking coming from the guest room. He went down to kiss her goodnight. He knocked on the door and heard she was on a phone call with her friends telling them about the eventful day she had. She motioned him to come in, which gave him time to just admire her even more. She was gorgeous, sad, happy, mad and scared. How could this be?

He continued to watch her as she ended the conversation by letting her friends know she would be leaving for New York in the morning and she had to get some rest. She said her goodbyes and stared directly into Mike's eyes.

He was again lost by her beauty. Moments went by

feeling like hours with no words but just silent language that only they understood.

She asked if he was okay? He told her he had never been better. She mentioned the shower and said that she was nervous, that things were moving too fast and she wasn't ready to go all the way.

Mike took her in his arms and told her that he would wait as long as she wanted him to as long as she was with him. Fear turned to relief as she laid protected in his arms. She knew that he was the man for her and that one day, hopefully, they could move into a forever relationship. She laid in his arms while he played in her hair until both of them fell off into a peaceful sleep.

Wilson sat in front of the big mansion of the famous Mike Keaton wondering what his next move was. The love of his life was behind that gate with the richest bachelor in the city when she should have been with him. When he saw her at the Walmart, she was even more beautiful up close which made him have to see what she was buying. He felt so connected to her. She was pretty, an athlete and a good worker and she belonged to him.

The security was extra tight at the mansion, meaning he needed another plan. Wilson left mad, defeated and feeling the need to kill another girl. He went home so that he could stalk his prey. He thought about how he must have to be more careful because he could have been caught at Walmart.

Mike woke up to notice Layla sleeping like an angel. He sat and watched her sleep, listened to her breathe a while, then went down to check on the rest of the family.

A Scared Life to a Loving Wife

The house was quiet and everyone was sound asleep.

Mike looked out and ensured that security was in place outside so he walked to the security office and realized John was on the cameras, flagging some footage. John told Mike that a suspicious car was sitting outside the gate for about 30 minutes and that he got the license plate number. Mike told him to give him an update, though he was going to bed to get some rest before flying out tomorrow. Mike went to his room and fell asleep thinking and dreaming about the angel who left heaven to make all his dreams come true.

14.
New York Here They Come

Layla was awakened by the smell of bacon cooking and her mom and sisters in the kitchen talking. Layla put on some shorts and went to join them. When she got to the kitchen her mom and Mike were talking over coffee while Tonya and Deidra were cooking with the maid and having a good time. It was amazing to see how the family got along with each other as if they'd known each other for years.

Her belly was growling, especially when she saw those pancakes, bacon and fruit. Layla spoke to everyone and kissed everyone and sat down on her mom's lap. Mike admired how beautiful all of these women were and how his future wife was so connected to her family. They had such an amazing relationship and he took a mental note on how he would love for her sisters to meet his cousins. He knew they would get along fine.

Layla got off her mom's lap and started fixing Mike a plate. She then fixed her family's plate before her own and then all of them bowed their heads to bless the food together. Layla's mom had done an amazing job with keeping them spiritually connected to God and the church. Mike took a mental note to visit the church more often. He thought it would be good if they found one they could all go together.

Everyone ate, talked and Layla reminded them of

A Scared Life to a Loving Wife

the trip to New York, which her mom thought was a great idea. Mike was very excited to show her around because she had never been on a plane or to New York. Time was moving fast so Layla ate and said that she would start getting dressed and bring her bags down.

Layla chose to wear a pair of tight blue jeans and a short sleeve shirt with a jacket. It was October so she figured that New York could be chilly. Layla packed seven outfits because Mike didn't give her an idea of how long they would be gone. An hour later Layla was dressed and had her bags at the door for the maid to put them in the car. Layla's hair was all curly since it had gotten wet the night before and she wasn't going to try to straighten it out.

She heard talking from a room down the hall so she proceeded to walk toward the voices. When she got to the room she noticed that Mike and John were in deep conversation and watching cameras. She excused herself to come in and John and Mike immediately stopped talking. That's when she noticed the car and recognized the car from the recreation center. Layla had shock on her face when she noticed that the stalker knew where she was. She told Mike and John that this was the same car that had been following her and watching her on the track.

Mike became furious. He told John to get on it and he grabbed his angel to comfort her and to tell her she had nothing to worry about, that John was the best and would get to the bottom of it. Mike's big strong arms swallowed her again and she felt protected.

He took her to his room to get his bags and called a

meeting with all security members letting them know what was going on and that they are to protect the house and the family with their own lives. Layla admired how good he was with leading and giving directions to others. He ordered the police officers to be paid and on duty at the mansion at all times. He looked at his watch and noticed that they had to be at the airport in one hour. The car was already waiting.

Layla went to say her goodbyes to her family and the security team walked them to the running car. Layla and Mike were on their way to the airport to go to New York to meet the famous Mr. and Mrs. Keaton whom she had heard so much about. Layla had no idea of the surprise that was waiting for her in New York but Mike knew all about it and couldn't wait to see it.

Layla and Mike arrived at Charlotte airport with about 30 minutes to spare, so Layla wanted to use the restroom. Mike walked her to it and waited outside the door to ensure her safety. Mike watched his surroundings and ensured his security team was in position. They were definitely on post and knew how to do their jobs well. Layla came out and Mike instructed Layla to stay with the guys while he went to the restroom with the other security worker. Layla had to get used to this because she was so independent and used to protecting herself, though apparently that wasn't good enough.

Mike was coming out of the restroom when two men and a woman at the door started talking to him and asking him for autographs. Layla was embarrassed for him. Security fell in line immediately. He did the

A Scared Life to a Loving Wife

autographs and made a beeline to Layla so that they could head to check in for their flight. The lady that got the autograph looked very disappointed that he wasn't alone. Layla wasn't bothered at all; she was used to the girls hating on her because of what she looked like, so this shouldn't be that different.

They got to check in and were able to skip the line because of Mike's status. Everyone knew how Mike rolled with his security team. Layla and the team were led to First Class where they would be the only ones in that area, which she was grateful for because this was a new experience for her. The flight attendant was very nice and flirtatious with the security team but never disrespected her with Mike. She offered food, beverages and wine which Layla was still not old enough to drink. Mike took a soda and held and kissed her hand. They stared in each other's eyes for what seemed like eternity, which caused Layla not to realize that they were already in the air. Layla realized that flying wasn't that bad and she could get used to it.

Mike continued to comfort her and then he kissed her on her lips. He then asked Layla if she was all his. Layla gave him a smile and said of course. He ran his fingers through her curly hair and told her how beautiful she was and that he wanted them to be exclusive. Layla smiled and said I thought we already were, which made Mike proud that his surprise was going to work in his favor.

After about one hour and thirty minutes later, they landed at Laguardia Airport in New York and walked to a stretched limousine with another security driver.

People were taking pictures of them already, but Mike didn't seem to mind as if he knew the environment already. Layla was nervous but she heard chatter in the crowd on how she was pretty and that they made a cute couple. She also heard haters doing what they do best because of course they wanted to be in her spot, but Layla took a mental note that she may need some training on getting used to all the attention and pictures.

The drive to his parents' house seemed to take a long time and Layla got a little nap. Finally, they rode up to a long driveway and into a gate with one of the biggest mansions Layla had ever seen. She thought Mike's mansion was huge, but this one was on an estate in its own world. There were gardeners, butlers and a team of maids working inside and out. Layla didn't think she could imagine a mansion like this one.

When the car stopped a beautiful woman and Mike's twin came out on the porch. Layla instantly got nervous and looked into the mirror to ensure she looked okay. She waited for her door to open and stepped out with Mike to greet his parents. They were very nice people. Layla assumed they would be snooty, but it was the total opposite. Mike kissed his mother, hugged his father and introduced Layla. They both immediately said they admired how beautiful she was. The mother said her name was June Keaton and the father said his name was Coal Keaton. Layla immediately put some respect in front of it and called them Mr. and Mrs. Keaton which got her a little favor with the parents.

A Scared Life to a Loving Wife

They invited her in and the mansion was gorgeous. Layla was able to get a tour of the house which had 16 bedrooms, 15 bathrooms, 3 kitchens and a guest house. There was a pool and jacuzzi room inside and outside, a library, workout room, and elevators. The only thing was missing was a map. Layla was scared of getting lost because the house had 4 levels to see. To give you an idea, the estate was bigger than the Biltmore and the White House. It was amazing. The maids prepared an awesome lunch. Mike gave Layla a tour of the guesthouse which had 4 bedrooms, 2 bathrooms and was very cozy. Layla was glad that she wouldn't be left alone on all those levels and thought the guesthouse was more of what she was used to.

Mike said that they could relax because there would be a fancy dinner tonight with some live music because he had a surprise. Layla was nervous because she didn't know what to expect with Mike and felt glad that she bought a fancy dress and some heels, always trying to be prepared. Layla decided that she would get her gown ready and call her family to tell them about the experience so far which was exciting. Mike was so tickled about how she wasn't used to the lifestyle and thought that she might want to start getting used to it because he had no plans in letting her get out of his sight.

She ended the phone call and started straightening her hair when Mike picked her up in his big strong arms and wouldn't let her go. He kissed her and then laid her head on his chest. Layla thought about how she was falling deeper and deeper in love with him and was scared at the same time. Mike remembered how he didn't want to move too fast, so he let her go with a silent gaze. Layla looked into his eyes to feel his mood and then realized it was the mood she wasn't prepared for.

She got up to do her hair while Mike watched her. In the meantime, Layla's mother and sisters were on a plane heading to New York because tonight was a night that Layla wouldn't forget. It was about 6 p.m., so Layla started to get dressed for dinner not knowing what to expect.

Mike had gone off into a separate room of the guesthouse when Layla thought it would be a good idea to take a bath. She was in there relaxing when she heard Mike on the phone with his parents telling them to "bring her at" 7:30 because they were here. Layla was trying to eavesdrop to find out who they were, so she hopped out, brushed her teeth, and started getting dressed.

Layla had a black formal gown that hugged all the right areas and her heels were black and silver, stiletto style which was perfect for the occasion. Layla's jewelry was on point and her hair was straight with Shirley Temple curls flowing down her back.

When she walked into the living room where Mike was dressed in a black tuxedo, and white shirt, she did not know that they would match so well. Layla was mesmerized by what she saw, and Mike was blinded by her beauty. Once the staring match was over, Mike informed her that a car would be there shortly to take them to the mansion where the party would be held.

A Scared Life to a Loving Wife

Layla wanted to know whose party it was and Mike just said that she would soon understand that his parents loved to have parties.

When the limo came Mike escorted Layla to the car, kissed her hand and closed the door before the driver could get out and complete his job task. The driver was able to be successful with Mike's door and they drove toward the main house. When they got to the mansion, she noticed that his parents had been very busy. There were people everywhere by the pool area and in the house. Layla didn't know too many of them. Everyone was dressed in fancy gowns and tuxedos and lots of them looked very well off.

Layla walked into the main kitchen and watched in awe at how big the table was and how many seats were decorated as if there would be a big crowd attending dinner tonight. Mike grabbed her hand and started taking her around to introduce her to their friends and family. Layla met Mike's younger sister, who was one year, one month and one day apart from him, something very unique. Her name was Nicole and she was such a sweet young lady. She managed the finances of her mother's business, which was a big job because they had so many. Mike also introduced Layla to his older brother Jeremy and his wife who lived in Denver. He had five daughters who were all very nicely mannered. He had three cousins whom Mike called brothers because they were very close. They all were business owners and were doing very well for themselves. One of his cousins was named Corey and he was close to Mike's age. Layla knew that Tonya would think that he was very attractive. He was also single, which was a plus. Layla recognized the two friends from the club and spoke to them. Layla found out that they also worked in the family business as well.

 Layla was about to be excused to the restroom when she heard some familiar voices. She heard her mother talking with Mrs. Keaton. Tonya and her sister Deidra were coming towards her. She was so glad that she had someone she knew there with her. She immediately grabbed Tonya and Deidra to go to the restroom with her to freshen up. They were heading toward one of the restrooms when she heard two other familiar voices which were her two best friends Lina and Jennifer. She was very happy because she had her main family there with her and didn't feel alone anymore.

 Layla had a lot of questions about when they arrived and how Mike pulled this off. Her friends told her that Mike told his friends to let them know that they were invited to the party in New York and that it was a surprise and that it was important for them to be there. Everyone had questions now, but Layla knew she needed to find Mike to get the answers.

 Her friend were bragging on how good she had it because he had paid for all their travel and arranged for a car to pick them up and said that their hotels were already paid for, as well. Mike was obviously extremely busy when she was sleeping, but she wasn't surprised because he had so many people who would do his work for him and he wouldn't miss a date with her.

A Scared Life to a Loving Wife

They were all coming down the steps when the maids started directing everyone in for dinner. Everyone moved towards the kitchen area so that they could be seated in the right spot. Layla and her friends weren't used to this but were very excited. Layla saw her mother who joined their group and then she saw Mike who was looking at her to make sure that she was okay.

The maid waited for Mike's parents to sit down, then started sitting everyone in a strategic order and sat them together at the head end of the table. Then she sat Layla's mother, sisters and friends close by and Mike's family was also sitting together. There was so much food: steak, lobster, shrimp, salad, fruit, sushi and even crab legs. Her family was just as excited as she was. Mike's parents really knew how to throw a party.

Everyone was trying to figure out what the occasion was, but nobody knew except her mother and Mike's parents. All the food was put on the tables and then Mr. Keaton asked if Layla's mother would bless the food. Her mom said that she would be honored. Layla loved to hear her mother pray. She was her hero and had a great relationship with God.

Her mom finished praying and Mrs. Keaton thanked her for that wonderful prayer. Out of nowhere, a man playing a violin came in playing "All of Me" by John Legend and it was beautiful. Layla froze, not knowing what to expect. She definitely wasn't expecting another man bringing a covered tray their way which caught everyone's attention as well. Mike stood and lifted the tray, grabbed something and went down on his knees while the song was playing softly. Layla covered her mouth and at the same time tried to hold the tears back. Her mother was already in tears along with her friends and her sisters.

Mike spoke, "Layla, I have loved you since the first day I saw you in the grocery store and I knew that I couldn't live without you. The timing was bad but I knew that you were made for me. Ever since then, I prayed, wrote poems on your beauty and asked God to let me see you again when the time was right so I could be complete. He did that on your 18th birthday. I knew that night that I didn't want to live another day without you in my life. You are an angel from heaven, which caused God to be short one angel, because you are here with me. I have already gotten your mother's permission and thanked her for raising such an elegant young lady for me. I know that you are young and still have things that you want to accomplish and I am willing to wait and be there with you to achieve your accomplishments. But, Layla, I am asking you to do me the honor of becoming my partner, my wife and the mother of my children. You are my rib and I don't want to live another day without you by my side, so please say yes."

Layla was shocked. She looked at all the happy faces around the table and how her life was about to change and how she loved Mike and "yes" came out of her mouth.

Mike stood and scooped her up. The crowd rose and clapped and everyone was wiping tears from their eyes. Sparkling grape juice was brought out to the table to

A Scared Life to a Loving Wife

celebrate and everyone ate and enjoyed the fellowship. They brought out so many different desserts as well.

Mike kissed Layla and thanked everyone for being a part of the celebration. He said for everyone to eat as much as they wanted to. Everybody ate while the live band played. Both families joined together in dance while enjoying the occasion. The whole party came over to congratulate them and looked at the ring. The ring was not only big but heavy. Layla thought how one day she would be Mrs. Keaton. Layla was in her own thoughts just thinking how a little, ordinary, black girl could fall in love with a rich man and could have anything that she ever dreamed of and more.

It was getting late in the evening and Mike had another busy day planned for Layla and her sisters so she needed plenty of rest. Layla was dancing with her sisters and best friends who were flirting with their new friends from the club. They had gotten very close and even in relationships. Layla looked around and noticed everyone just having a good time in their own world. Tonya was talking to Mike's cousin, whom she knew that she would like, so this was going the way it should go.

Evening turned to night and everyone had started to say their goodbyes to do their own thing. Layla sat watching Mike talk to some of his family and friends and was getting very tired. Mike noticed that his fiancée was tired and decided to take her back to the guest house. He said goodnight to all his family and then Mike grabbed his fiancée's hand and led her to the car opening the door for his queen to be. Layla felt so spoiled around Mike but little did she know she hadn't seen anything yet.

Layla and Mike got back to the guest house and as soon as she got in Mike embraced her with a hug and was caressing her curves in that dress. He told her that he had wanted to do that all day, but didn't want to mess up anything because she had looked so angelic. Layla laughed and reciprocated the mood by embracing him back, looking at Mike in his eyes and saying that she loved him. Mike and Layla kissed and Mike wanted to know if she felt like talking to him a little while. They sat and talked and shared things about one another so there wouldn't be any secrets. He wanted to know everything about her and he wanted her to know him as well. He wanted to spend his whole life making her happy. Hours went by and they were both getting tired because it had been a long, exciting day.

Layla decided to change into something more comfortable while Mike was in the bathroom doing the same thing. Layla came out of the guest room and saw Mike in the other room with the door closed so she went and opened the door without knocking. Layla caught Mike in the nude. Layla's eyes grew big and she was so embarrassed that she didn't knock first. She loved the view which gave her that feeling in her stomach. Mike turned around and watched her watching him. He looked like something straight from a model video. Mike was not lacking in any department, which instantly turned Layla on. Layla apologized and closed her eyes but she felt him

A Scared Life to a Loving Wife

embracing her which wasn't helping her mentally with her struggles.

Layla still wasn't ready so she excused herself to let him put on some clothes. Mike wanted her so badly but he knew that he would wait as long as she needed to be comfortable and ready to share her complete body with him. Mike put on his clothes and met Layla into the living room area where they cuddled. He played in her curls and scratched her back causing Layla to fall asleep in Mike's strong arms.

15.
Something New

Layla woke up and felt rejuvenated. She didn't have any nightmares. She remembered having dreams of Mike and her having a pretty daughter who looked much like a mixture of them and smiled knowing that she was having those dreams after having such an amazing day. She noticed that she was in the room she was in when she first got there, meaning Mike must have carried her to the bedroom after she fell asleep.

She went out to get refreshed because it was already about 9 in the morning. She didn't know what the plans were, but she did remember that her best friends said that they would be here another day, so maybe they could all go explore the city.

She heard Mike in his room moving around and then she heard a knock on the guesthouse door. Layla went to ask who it was but was able to look into the peep hole and see the maids bringing breakfast to the guest house. She let them in and they went to the kitchen area with all types of pastries, grits and fruit. They also had coffee and orange juice.

Layla was kind of hungry and then she saw Mike coming out of the room to head towards the kitchen area. He stopped and kissed her on the lips. He waited until she sat down and then went to his chair. He blessed the food and they started eating as if they were already a happy family. Layla thought about how one day there would be more people included in their

A Scared Life to a Loving Wife

family which would be their beautiful children.

Mike and Layla talked about the plans for today, which was to hang out with her friends and family before her friends leave to go back home. After breakfast the security car was already out front waiting for them. Layla waited for Mike open the door to let her in and then he got in and they were off to the city.

They rode to a fancy hotel not too far from the estate and in jumped Lina and Jennifer who were already excited to be hanging out in the Big Apple. The car rode around and ended up in an area where there were a lot of shopping places. Mike watched the excitement on his fiancée's and friends' faces when they realized that this was shopping heaven. They hopped out and the security driver and Mike followed along where Mike planned to buy Layla and her friends whatever they wanted.

Layla and her friends had never been treated like this, though Mike thought that they deserved it. All of these women were smart and were used to getting things on their own, but he wanted to show his appreciation of their attendance and acceptance of him marrying their best friend one day soon. The girls shopped and ate. About 2 p.m. they grew tired and were ready to go back to their hotel.

They were getting up with his friends a little later. Mike had talked to them. His boys were really glad that they met Layla's friends. Everyone had things in common and they were looking forward to taking their friendships to another level as well.

The car pulled back up at their hotel and Layla got

out to hug her friends and say her goodbyes. The girls wanted to also again congratulate her for being engaged and they expressed how happy they were for her.

Mike wasn't done with spoiling his queen for that day. He still had other surprises that he wanted to fulfill. They rode in another area where there was a store that sold jewelry that he wanted to look in. Layla wasn't a big jewelry lover, but she would follow Mike to Mars and back if he asked her to. They walked around and Mike talked to the owner, who went into the back to retrieve two boxes. In the boxes were matching sets for them which included a bracelet saying His Queen and Her King and a necklace that matched when you put them together that formed a heart that said that I Love You. She thought the gifts were so thoughtful, but the price seemed outrageous. Mike put the bracelet and necklace on Layla and she did the same with Mike's. They were officially a matching set with the engagement ring, and matching bracelet and necklace.

Mike thought it would also be nice if they got some pampering done as well, so he took her to an upscale massage parlor that did it all including nails, feet, eyebrows, hair and massages. Layla opted to do the massage and pedicure but she didn't trust the hair dresser. She only allowed Felicia, to do her hair. She had been doing her hair for years and she was very loyal to her. The only other backup she would allow to do her hair was Rhonda which was the other hair stylist that owned the salon. They were also her friends and family and they both knew how to get it done. She made a note that when she got back in town she would call Felicia to make an appointment to get her hair washed and straightened.

After Mike and Layla got their massages and pedicures it was getting about dinner time and decided that they would go to a restaurant with good steak. They ended up at an upscale restaurant sort of like Ruth's Chris, though the food was much more expensive in New York. Dreams were discussed, along with her plans of the ideal career in the medical field. The food and service were amazing and the waitress Mia was the best in the world. Mike gave her a hefty tip, which caused Mia to be moved to tears.

After dinner, it was time to go back to the estate and maybe see what her mother and sisters were up to. When they got back, her mother and sisters were still enjoying themselves with Mike's parents. They were even talking about health things and what her mom's dreams were that she wanted to do in the medical world. Her mom shared that she loved to nurse, but would also love to go into the administration part of nursing. She would be willing to relocate because she never had lived anywhere else but North Carolina.

Layla was happy to know what her mom's true ambitions were. Layla was smart, just like her mother. Her mom had done an amazing job raising her and her sisters alone, even with her no-good boyfriend her mother had done very well. Layla thought about how, when her mother was married to her daddy, she still wasn't happy. Now it was time for her to find happiness in her own life, especially since the girls were able to take care of themselves now.

It was definitely another long day that she would not remember and she was ready to go get some rest at last. Layla talked with her family and her new extended family for a while and decided to go back to the guest house to go to sleep. Mike was on a phone call that sounded important so Layla thought to give him some privacy.

They had already been in New York for a couple of days and she was liking the environment. It didn't hurt that a lot of good memories were here and Mike's family was also here, so she kept that in mind as well. She went into her bedroom and laid across the bed and it seemed like she was able to fall right to sleep.

Mike was on the phone talking with John checking to see where the case was and if any new information had come out about the recent events at home. The police had discovered that the police officer found dead was killed by strangulation but there were no suspects, and the girl who was dead was also raped and discovered in the dumpster at some dorm apartments at a local college. They believed the murders could be related because the college girl and the cop had an ongoing relationship, so the investigation was continuing. They believed that a dark colored, four door car was at the scene of both and were asking anyone with information to contact the local police department. The police were unsuccessful with getting the tag number to the car, however they thought that the killer was from the area and maybe could be on

A Scared Life to a Loving Wife

campus or related to it. They had put an alert for the local colleges to be on high alert until they were able to get more information on the motive and to rule out if the rapist and killer could be on campus or not.

Mike ended the call with John and looked for his angel, whom he found sleeping so peacefully in her room. Mike thought he would lay with her so that she would wake up beside him. He couldn't wait until they could sleep together every night. He knew that he was not able to keep his hands off of her because it was just too tempting. So he just watched her, played in her hair and rubbed and kissed her pretty face. She didn't wake up, so he went to his room and fell asleep thinking how he couldn't wait until the day that she walk down that aisle to be the official Mrs. Keaton.

16.
Six Months Later...Fresh Meat at College

Layla definitely had an exciting summer, but it was time to jump into the school world and get back to working out. She had been spending so much time with Mike spoiling her that she wasn't going to the track like she used to. Mike and Layla decided that, with everything going on, living on campus might not be as safe. They had not yet caught the killer. Mike was very overprotective and said, if she decided to live on campus, a security guard would have to go everywhere she went. Layla thought that living on campus would be even weirder.

Layla was just excited to be in her first year of college. She was able to meet the track team and the coach and everyone seemed easy to get along with. Layla and her two best friends were just glad to see each other at the same school. Jennifer and Lina decided to still be roommates and Layla hung out and studied with them a lot. Mike and Layla still spent a lot of time together and Mike even pressured her a little more about marrying him sooner. Layla didn't want to complicate things with school and being a wife.

Life was great with her family. Her mom decided to take an administrator job in one of Mike's dad's hospitals and her sisters were both in committed relationships with good jobs. Mike's parents kept in touch with them and also asked when they could expect to be planning a wedding. Layla let them know that she was focusing on her freshman year. They talked about a wedding for next year.

Layla was a catch on campus. However it was easy for her to turn guys away because she had that big rock on her finger. When she told them who her fiancé was, everyone seemed to respect his territory because he and his family were well known around the campus. Mike still didn't like that his fiancée was getting hit on daily and decided that he would talk to her about doing online classes. He didn't want her to know that he was a little jealous.

Mike was doing a lot of different projects for his parents and he was also writing another book. He seemed to have a lot to write about these days because she was his inspiration and he could write about her everyday. Layla loved to work out on Wake's track. It was a lot larger, but she loved to run on it. Layla was working out on the track when she noticed a group of people sitting on the bleachers. There were two girls and two boys. Layla thought that maybe they were athletes. They commented on Layla on her skills on the track.

Then she noticed a guy watching her from the top of the hill. His frame looked very familiar. She knew that it was not the security guard, but there was something creepy about him watching her. She immediately tried to alert the security. It seemed as if he wasn't aware of what was happening. Layla's heartbeat started to speed up and she felt a panic attack coming on.

She reached into her pocket, grabbed her phone and called Mike. He listened to her breathing and started to talk to her and calm her down, letting her know that he was already in route to her because he had a feeling something wasn't right. The security guard was heading her way when Mike came down the steps and put her in his arms. Layla pointed in the direction of where the guy was standing but no words were coming out of her mouth. She noticed that the guy was not there anymore. Layla was so upset that she was not able to describe the guy well enough that the security guard or Mike could catch him.

Mike took Layla home so that maybe she could do a description for John and the police officer. His first priority was to get her home safe, because he wouldn't know what he would have done if something happened to the only woman that he had ever loved.

17.
Wilson's Dream Come True

Wilson sat admiring her from the track, but noticed that she wasn't alone. She was going to be hard to get by herself because in order to do that he was going to have to get rid of this security guard that she always had with her. That wasn't going to be easy on a college campus. For now, he would stand around and enjoy watching her do what she loved to do: run track and run him crazy in his own mind. She was the most beautiful girl that he had ever seen. He thought about going down and getting a little closer but decided that would be risky being that he was supposed to just be the maintenance man and not an actual student. The more he watched her the more in love he became with her. He needed to do something to get her to notice him or would that be also too risky? What if she remembers his face from the club or the Walmart or even the funeral! He was so connected to her because they had history together.

He was in his own thoughts that he didn't realize that she was watching him watching her. Wilson took off towards the maintenance room on campus and stayed put until the coast was clear. He saw the famous Mike come to her side with more security and take her away to the car. Mike was beginning to make him mad because he was spending too much time with the woman that was supposed to be his. He was definitely a distraction and he might need to get him out of the way first so that he could take what was his and nobody else's.

Wilson noticed that the coast was clear so he locked the maintenance room up and went to his room on campus to come up with a plan to get closer to his dream-come-true. He sat down and looked into his scope to see if anyone looked worth taking. Then he realized the only one he wanted was her. He got into deep thought of what she would smell like, how would she taste. The thought of making love to her caused Wilson to start doing his normal when he thought about her. She had some serious effects on him, even making him think that he wouldn't have to kill anymore. The thoughts of settling down and maybe even having a child or two. The thoughts of children came and left at the same time because he knew the world didn't need another like himself thanks to his sick, deceased father. Just marrying her whether she wanted to or not would be enough to make all his dreams come true.

17.
His Nightmare

Layla and Mike got back to the mansion and Mike wanted to talk with Layla about maybe doing online classes or taking more security. Layla just wanted to relax so she went to run a jacuzzi bath and added some bubbles. She was taking off her clothes when Mike came in and asked if he could talk with her.

Layla already had given the police the sketch of the guy she saw, which was the same guy she remembered from the Walmart. Why did she seem to have a stalker? What did he want with her? This was not the time in her life where she needed to have fear. She was just getting used to the campus and the track team and wanted everything to be okay.

Mike was talking to her about online classes and this was not what Layla wanted for her college life. She felt that Mike was overreacting and being controlling so she told him that she was going back to school because she wasn't going to live in fear of a possible stalker. Mike noticed that Layla was getting upset and he didn't want to be the cause of another panic attack so he told her to do as she wished, that he only wanted her to be safe and happy.

Layla finished her bath and thought that she would call her friends over so that they could be supportive and help her make the right decision. Jennifer and Lina came right over and were very supportive. Layla told them about the possible stalker and they said that nobody would bother their friend and that she should still come to the campus because she had security and everything would be fine. Layla agreed and decided that she would go back to campus the next day to her classes and to the track and practice with the rest of the team. The team was just starting to know who she was and liking the skills that she had. She wanted to possibly make more friends on the track. She prayed about it and decided that going back to school was what she was going to do.

Layla and Mike saw her friends out and Layla decided to get in the bed so that she could make it on time for class tomorrow. She went to her room and Mike said that he loved her and decided to go to sleep.

Mike was sleeping when he was awakened by a horrible dream that Layla was missing and he didn't know where she was. He was doing all he could to find her, but she didn't show up. Mike woke up from the dream sweating and feeling around for her. He went to her room and there she was sleeping like an angel. He got in the bed next to her, put her in his arms and fell asleep and slept like a king. Layla continued to sleep peacefully and felt protected and safe again in Mike's arms.

She woke up and was glad that it was Friday. She only had two classes today and afterwards could hit the track early and head home. Mike said that he wanted to take her out to dinner that night so she was looking forward to having a nice dinner with her fiancé.

Layla did her last class and thought that she would

go to the girl's locker room to change into her workout clothes for the track. The security guy was standing outside the locker room respecting her privacy, so Layla went in. The locker room was empty so she used the restroom and was changing her clothes when she heard someone in the stall beside her. Somebody must have come in through the other entryway away from the door she came in.

Layla got an eerie feeling and decided to come out. When she walked out she was held in a strong set of arms with a hand over her mouth. Layla was fighting to get free but she felt a little poke in her arm and everything started to get dark. The man who was holding her picked her up and left through the door away from the door the security guard was standing at. He put her in a car and took her away from the campus.

About twenty minutes had gone by and the security guard started getting a little nervous. He wanted to respect the women's bathroom so he looked around and saw two other students going into the bathroom. He politely asked them to look for a girl that had gone in about twenty minutes ago and gave a description. The girls seemed happy to help and went in to look around. When they came out they told him that nobody was there, however there was a bag in the changing room. The security guard came into the locker room grabbed the bag and immediately got on the phone with Mike and John who got the news and were enroute to the campus. They also alerted the police and campus police. Mike was able to bring a picture and tell the police what she had on and the last place that she was seen.

Mike's nightmare had come true, his true love was missing and he believed that it was her stalker that took her. Mike felt sick. He called his parents and they said that they would make some phone calls and would be on the next plane to North Carolina. Mike was in his own world. There were questions after questions and Mike told the authorities about the guy who had been watching her and showed them the picture.

The campus was put on lockdown and the picture of Layla and the possible suspect was put on the news. Some of the girls on campus knew who the guy was and said that he was the head of the maintenance department and did seem a little weird. Word got around fast on campus. Lina and Jennifer were devastated and angry. Their best friend had possibly been abducted and the man who did it could be the one responsible for the other murders in the state.

Mike contacted Layla's mother and sisters, who were already on their way because it was breaking news. Layla's mother and sisters were crying and very upset. Tonya was able to tell them again about the guy in Walmart and to do a sketch which confirmed that this could be the same man. Tonya was sick on her stomach because this was a sick man who seemed to be fixated on her sister.

While it was crazy on campus Wilson was very calm in his house. He took her to the house he grew up in. He thought the basement would be good because nobody would hear her just in case she got up and started screaming. He was able to admire her while she was out. He gave her a mild sedative so she should be waking up very soon. He taped her mouth and laid her on the bed with her hands and feet in restraints. He didn't want to restrain her but, when she woke up, he knew that she would probably be startled and scream and he couldn't risk that.

Layla started to move around, meaning the medicine was wearing off. Wilson put his black covering over his face but he watched as she woke up like Sleeping Beauty. She kicked and fought to try to get her hands free, but she was not successful. Wilson tried to calm her down by running his fingers through her hair and letting her know that he didn't want to hurt her.

Layla was a fighter. She fought and fought and gave him a look of disgust. She was even beautiful, scared and mad. She got quiet and started to beg him to let her go. She already wanted to go. He desired her to need and want him. Did she not feel the same for him? Layla was angry and he could tell that she wanted to fight him.

He told her that, if she wouldn't scream, he would take the mouth tape off. She agreed that she wouldn't scream but she wanted to know why he was doing this to her. Wilson told her that she was his and that they had history together and he couldn't let her be with anyone else. He let her know that he took her ring off because he had a ring for her and that she belonged to him and not the famous Mike Keaton.

Layla looked confused and then asked him to show his face. Wilson was scared to show his face so soon. He told her that he would when the time was right. He also told her that they would be leaving the state soon so that nobody could stop them from being together.

Layla realized that she was being held against her will by a guy that had been following her practically all her life. All the thoughts ran through her head of how she kept running into this guy and how he had been watching her and how he could be the killer that the police were looking for. Layla thought about how when Mike asked her to go to school from home and the argument they had the night before because she wanted to do things her way and didn't want the extra security. She wanted to be a regular college student and just run track.

Layla was defeated. She knew that her mother and sisters would be very worried and whether or not she would be able to escape. Layla looked around to try to see something that could help her find out where she was, but the room was dark, cold and gloomy. There was one window, but the glass seemed to be extra thick so that nobody could hear anything coming out of it.

Layla was beginning to panic. What if nobody found her before they left the state? Was her life about to end and she did not even get the opportunity to become Mrs. Keaton? Layla felt her chest getting heavy and she started to feel really dizzy. She couldn't remember when she last ate or drank something, but a panic attack was on the rise. Layla felt that she wasn't getting enough oxygen and, before she knew it, she had passed out.

It seemed like hours had passed before Layla came back to reality. When she opened her eyes, he was just

A Scared Life to a Loving Wife

staring at her like he had his prize out of the cracker jack box. Layla asked him to please let her go and that she wouldn't say a word.

The guy seemed confused. He looked at her and asked her, "Why don't you love me like I love you? You are my angel and my life and I never stopped loving you!"

Now it was Layla's time to look confused. He then told her that he was her first and that he never meant to hurt her and that the other man that had her was now dead because she was supposed to have been all his. He admitted and apologized for the girl that was killed and told her that it was because he was thinking about her and was mad that she had found someone else. He admitted to being the one that was in the front seat when his dad used to take her mom around and that he knew his love was real when he saw her at his father's funeral. He admitted being the one that even saw her on her birthday, but she didn't notice him because of the famous Mike Keaton. He claimed that he was only looking after her and that she never seemed to notice him but now she will. He said that he took her in order for her to notice him so that they could be together and start a family.

Layla had tears of fear, sorrow and fury in her eyes. A part of her wanted to break out and kill him herself and another part wanted to find out what made him this person, whom she wanted to help—though killing him sounded better because he got her locked up and had admitted to killing the other two people. So fight-flight was definitely a must in her current situation.

Layla knew she would have to play her cards right if she wanted to live. There was no time to make any mistakes. Layla first apologized for not noticing him and said that she wasn't trying to be mean to him but that they should use this time to get to know each other better. She noticed that his demeanor got more relaxed and he wasn't on the defense. He seemed to like her ideas, which meant that reverse psychology was working. Layla asked him to talk about his childhood.

Layla could feel the shift in the mood when she mentioned his childhood. Wilson told her that it was horrible and that all he was able to do was to stay in this room and listen while his father brought a lot of different women home to have his way with them, some of whom he never saw again. He said that he loved his mother but was told by his father that she had abandoned them and wasn't coming back. He then told his mother was later found dead and the police ruled it as an overdose, although he felt that his father had something to do with it because his mother wasn't a user. He said that he was glad that his father was dead and at least his parents had left him with a nice insurance policy which would help them to live happily ever after.

Layla listened to him and then asked him, "So why did you have to do that to me?"

Wilson started to blank out and beat himself upside the head and act like a child having a tantrum. She calmed him down by reaching for his hand and rubbing it as much as she could. He immediately came out of that trance and went into another trance watching her

A Scared Life to a Loving Wife

rub his hand. Layla then noticed that something else was also coming alive so she stopped rubbing his hands. He was psychotic and she didn't want to give him any other ideas.

Layla changed the subject and asked what time it was. Wilson told her it was 7:30 p.m. Layla realized that she had been held hostage for longer than six hours. She watched shows that mentioned if a woman is abducted, authorities have 48 hours to find them alive. Layla was trying to beat the odds because she had too much to live for. She needed a plan and she needed it fast.

She mentioned that she was getting hungry and she would really like to be able to use the restroom and if he could at least undo the handcuffs. She promised that she wouldn't run.

Wilson said that he didn't trust her yet. He would let her go to the restroom but he would stay outside the door. Layla figured to take what she could get, which would still give her a moment to look around and find out where she was.

Wilson walked her down a hall to a door. When she came out the dark room she noticed that she was in an old house. There was a staircase to the right which probably led to the upper part of the house. This basement was finished with a den, kitchen and a bar. The house didn't seem to be in bad shape, but it felt very eerie and it was also cold and uncomfortable.

He walked her in and told her that she had ten minutes after which he would come in after her. She still had the handcuffs on so she begged for five more minutes since she would have to do all she needed to do in handcuffs. He said okay he would compromise with his love and that he wasn't hard to get along with at all.

Layla went into the bathroom and looked around. There was a window above the toilet and she wanted to get a closer look. She shut the door and turned on the water to make some noise. Layla quietly opened drawers looking for anything that she could use as a weapon. She climbed on top of the toilet and looked out the window. She was able to see other houses and diagonally across the street she could see the set apartments that she used to live in.

Panic jumped in her chest because he was able to watch her and that is how she was snatched as a child. She realized that he had been stalking and watching her for years and now he believed that he was part of her life. Layla flushed the toilet and acted as if she was using the restroom, but she was trying to see how high the window was, which wasn't high at all because they were in a basement.

Layla began to have a little hope. Layla looked in the cabinet and found a fingernail file. She hid it in her clothes for later use.

She was washing her hands again when he came in to see what she was doing. She smiled at him and told him she could be trusted. She asked what they were going to eat. She was getting hungry and hadn't eaten since the run at school. Wilson asked her what type of pizza she wanted and that he would go and order a pizza and would be right back. Layla told him that

A Scared Life to a Loving Wife

would be fine and that she would be waiting.

Wilson left out and shut the door. As soon as he shut that door Layla went to work on trying to get the handcuffs off. She was using the fingernail file to pick the lock which she saw done on a tv show. This wasn't easy at all for someone who was not a criminal, but she had to keep trying. She could hear Wilson on the phone with someone and figured he was ordering the pizza so she kept working.

Layla said a quiet prayer that God would give her the strength to get loose and that she would forever be grateful. God answered her prayers because she heard a click and one of the handcuffs came off. Layla kept working with the other and just like that her hands were free.

Layla ran to the room and hid behind the door so that, when he came back, she would be ready to fight. She saw a lamp on the dresser so she took the lamp to make the room dark so that it would give her a little advantage. Layla's heart was beating very fast because she knew she only had one chance to get away. She stood behind the door and waited for him to come back in. She heard him hanging up the phone and coming towards the room.

Layla waited for him to open the door and walk towards the room when she hit him in the head with the lamp. Wilson fell to the floor and Layla stepped hard in his growing area and came down with the fingernail file and stabbed him in the eye. She started toward the door when he grabbed her leg. Layla gave him a kick with her strong track legs and she took off up the steps to the top of the house. Layla got up the steps, closed the door and put the lock on it. She grabbed the phone from the charger took off towards the front door. She called the police and noticed that the deadbolt was on the front door so she ran to the kitchen area where she could open the door.

She heard Wilson banging on the door which meant that he had made it to the top of the steps. Layla was out the back door in a flash, telling the police she was on the run and had been with the killer who they were looking for. Layla told them she didn't know the street name but the apartment was known as Happy Hills Gardens and she was going to run until she found someone to help her. She noticed the more she ran the closer she got to familiar territory.

She ran past her apartments to her old friend Shenika's house where her mother was always at home. She knocked and Ms. Bailey let her in. She wanted to talk but noticed that Layla didn't have any shoes on and not enough clothes, so she immediately got on the phone to call the police as well and gave them her address. Ms. Bailey didn't play any games. She locked the door, told Layla to hide and went into her room to get her gun. She didn't know whether he was following her or not or whether he was in a car driving to find her, but Ms. Bailey waited on the police and called Layla's mother and told her that she was here and needed some help.

Layla's mother relayed the message to everyone. The search party headed her way to help. Mike was relieved and nervous at the same time and had prayed

A Scared Life to a Loving Wife

that the love of his life wasn't hurt. The security team and Mike were gone in a flash heading towards the action. Layla was relieved but still very nervous at the same time. Layla started hearing sirens and felt that she was a little closer to safety but that's when she saw the blue station wagon riding down the street. She hid and told Ms. Bailey it looked like his car and that's when all the police started to come but not before they started chasing the station wagon down into the neighborhood.

There were cops everywhere, flooding the neighborhood. With Mike and the team and others from the school they were able to put a face with the car and knew who they were chasing. He had his pictures on the news and everyone was watching for him. The police even offered a cash prize to anyone who knew where to find him. College students had taken the authorities to the dorm room and told them that he was the maintenance man and was a weird guy. It didn't take long at all for other cops to raid his house where he had kept the victims.

Layla felt relieved. She noticed some familiar cars and knew that it was her family, Mike and the security team. The ambulance arrived, asking her if she was hurt and there were lots of cops wanting to know what happened.

The cops had caught Wilson and he went straight to jail. Layla breathed a sigh of relief because she didn't want him to be able to hurt another girl or stalk her anymore. Layla told the cops everything even about him admitting to her that he was the one who raped her when she was younger, and that he killed that cop who was the friend of his, who was his second rapist, and the other girl out of rage. She even told the cops how he had been following her for years and that he was obsessed with her.

Mike pulled up and Layla ran to his arms and Mike looked at his angel to see if he saw any damage. He wouldn't let her go and he thanked God that she was brought back safely. Layla waited for her mother and sisters and saw them coming with her two best friends.

The news crews were there recording live because this was a big thing in the small city. To add to matters she was Mike Keaton's future wife and everyone wanted a piece of the story. Mike's parents had made it into town and they were all there as well to support their son who was on the verge of losing it and firing some people from the security team. Layla was exhausted and was still hungry. It seemed as if the cops wanted to keep asking the same questions and she didn't have enough strength to make it through all of the excitement.

Tonya arrived and hugged her along with her mother, and Deidra prayed with her, thanking God for giving his strength and for being on her side. Mike came around and told the crew to get her something to eat and drink and go to the house and that they could finish the questions at another time or to come to their mansion where they stayed because his fiancée was tired and needed to rest.

The cops agreed that it had been a long day so they gave Mike a card and told Layla that, if she remembered anything else, to come to the station or call and a policeman would meet her at their home. Mike grabbed his family and the news crews were on Mike asking questions. Mike told the news that he was glad that the killer and stalker was caught and that his fiancée was safe and then he thanked the authorities and all the people who gave information on getting the stalker and killer caught while walking back to the car with security on his heels.

It was a quiet ride back to the mansion because everyone was in their own thoughts. Mike just held her. Layla was glad that she didn't have to talk about it right then, but she knew that she would tell him all about it when she digested the events herself.

Everyone got back to the mansion and Mike had a steak dinner waiting for everyone. Layla was so ready to eat but first she had to take a shower to try to wash off the dirty feeling of being locked up in a killer/stalker's basement.

Layla ran the water, put some bubble bath in and some Epsom salt because she wanted to just relax. She took off her clothes and got into the water and closed her eyes.

Her thoughts immediately turned to the events that had transpired that day. She was relieved that the killer was caught, but disgusted at the fact that the guy was also her rapist and stalker. She thought about how innocent he looked when he talked about how he missed his mother and how bad his father treated him, which was probably the cause of how sick and twisted he was in the first place. Layla started to feel sorry for him and thought about how many others didn't get a fair chance and what may have happened if they would have gotten help or talked with a psychologist.

Layla realized that she had a passion to help people and how she definitely knew that this was the area she could work in. She realized that when she helped someone else it took her troubles away and she gained satisfaction with helping someone else self-assess their own problems, which were steps with finding a solution.

Layla then thought about how the events could have been different only if she would have listened to her fiancé about getting the extra security or maybe doing some online classes instead of in person. Layla realized that she had a lot of choices she had to make or change in her life after this event and one was maybe marrying her fiancé sooner than later. She realized tomorrow is not promised and her life could have ended robbing her of the opportunity to give Mike what he wanted most in his life. She felt that she would relax, eat with her family and sleep on it and then she wanted to sit and tell Mike everything so that she could not let this situation ruin her life but be able to move on in spite of the fear of ever being stalked again.

18.
Facing Reality

Layla didn't remember when she went to sleep but when she woke up she was laying on Mike's chest and he was holding her tightly as if he never wanted to let her go. Moving must have startled him because he looked down at her and told her good morning, and asked how did she sleep? She smiled and told him that the sleep was wonderful and that if they could just spend time together and do some talking. Layla went to the front door to look out and noticed that people were outside the gate trying to get in to talk about yesterday's events. Layla realized that this probably would be her new normal and didn't want to deal with it. Mike came out and noticed the cars and got the security team on it so that they wouldn't be harassing his fiancée. Layla figured it would be best if they stayed in because she wasn't really in the mood for questions.

She did want to get her hair done so she called her hairdresser and asked if she would come to the house to do her hair because she couldn't get out at the moment. Felicia was always so dedicated. She said that she would head right over and to give her an hour to get the hair supplies from the shop. Felicia was the best there was out there. You didn't have to wait long to get your hair done and if your appointment was set you are going to be in that chair at that time. She did Layla hair and all her family and friends and she knew what to do and how to do it.

Felicia worked with another girl named Rhonda who was just as good. They were friends, worked very well together and had a shop on the southside which stayed jumping with customers. They were both God sent and she knew that she would always be loyal to her.

The maid was cooking something that smelled good and Layla told Mike that her hairdresser would be coming over shortly and to prepare enough food. He told her there would be plenty and to tell Felicia to come to the back and the security would let her in so that the News crew wouldn't notice. Layla texted Felicia the address and told her to come around the back and the security would let her in.

Layla didn't know that Mike had already called the spa team to come over and give her a massage and pedicure. He wanted them to totally relax because she had been through a tough time, and he wanted her to know that he would always protect her.

Layla went upstairs to put on some lounge clothes and was a little nervous about how the conversation would go between Mike, though she realized that Mike had always been a good listener and her anxiety started to go away.

Layla heard a female's voice downstairs and realized that Mike and Felicia were having a conversation. She came downstairs so they could eat and then get started. Breakfast was delicious and she was ready to get that hair done. Layla decided to just

A Scared Life to a Loving Wife

get it washed and get some Shirley Temples, which would last her for about a week or two.

Mike watched as the hairdresser did his fiancée's hair. He just admired how beautiful she was and wondered how he got so lucky. He couldn't wait to marry her.

Her family was out doing their own thing because he knew that he wanted to spend the day with her and talk with her to see how she was doing mentally. He decided to have a therapist on standby just in case it was too much for Layla to handle. His parents wanted them to come back and stay at the estate to get her away from the city, but he knew he must see how she was doing so that he wouldn't make any hasty decisions without talking with her first. It was the weekend and he wanted time to see how she was going to adjust to getting back into her regular routine but he knew that he would have to take one day at a time.

Mike paid Felicia really well and was letting her out the door when the spa team came in. Layla's eyes lit up and she looked really surprised that Mike still made plans, even though they were in the house. Mike and Layla both enjoyed manicures, pedicures and full body massages and Layla felt very relaxed.

The security team let the spa team out and they were both still lying down relaxed on the tables looking at each other in love. Layla sat up and went over to Mike. She grabbed his hand and led him to the living room so that they could start their conversation.

Layla told him everything. Some things she said through tears, but they needed to be said. She told Mike how Wilson admitted to raping her and following her since she was younger. It was like he had a connection to her and it wasn't neutral. Mike was so upset that he couldn't kill Wilson himself, but he listened to how his fiancée was still empathetic about Wilson explaining his childhood events and how he was a victim as well.

Mike listened and was glad that Layla was a fighter and was smart enough to get away from Wilson because it could have been so much worse. Both of them thought about the same thing, which was not being able to see each other again and how much they loved each other. Layla apologized for not letting him do what would have been best for her by having more security. She promised that she would do better with allowing him to make the better decisions for both of them. Mike was glad that she understood his feelings and his position in their relationship.

Layla said that she had been thinking about being married sooner because she didn't want anything else to come in between their relationship. She said she knew that he could be getting tired of waiting on her. Mike told her that it was her choice and he would love to be with her totally. So she said that she would love to get married sooner.

Mike was the happiest man on earth that she would finally be all his. He told her to pick a date and that he would have a team to make it happen. They picked April 16 of the following year. He realized that the date was less than 8 months away and so he decided to let everyone know and to get his team working on it.

19.
Five Months Later...Busy Bee

A lot had happened in five months, including Layla turning 19, doing school online, being a friend and sister and planning her big wedding with lots and lots of help. Everyone was very excited about being a part of a big wedding. The destination was set, including the time and the food for the wedding guests. The wedding planners were great and very professional. Mike's parents wanted it to be perfect because he was their only son.

Layla was getting more excited and nervous everyday, but she kept focusing on how happy she would be after making one of the biggest decisions in her life. Mike's father asked Layla's mother if he could walk her down the aisle and Tonya agreed that it would be fine. Tonya was doing well with her new job and had even decided that she was going to move on with her life by dating Mike's cousin. She was thinking about moving closer to the cousin that she had gotten serious with. Both of her friends had gotten proposals and had set dates for the following year and everyone was happy. Layla didn't know how she was this lucky, that one man changed everything and everyone around her.

Everything was set and she even had all of her needs including the dress and accessories. She had already talked with Felicia and Rhonda who were going to travel with the party to do hair and makeup and to ensure that she would always look good for the cameras. Mike seemed to be making all the plans for her as if he was the bride, which Layla didn't mind at all. She was going to just focus on showing up and being the bride.

Layla had a lot on her mind but her thoughts would sometimes wander back to the nightmare and how she still felt sorry for her stalker. He was going to be in jail for life because police were able to prove that he did the murders and kidnapping and the rape. He was never going to get out. Layla thought many times of going down to see him to forgive him so that she could heal and move on. She was still not ready. Maybe she could go with Mike for support so that she wouldn't be scared. For right now, Layla would just focus on showing up, not passing out, and being Mike's bride.

Layla was deep in thought when Mike came in and told her that the hotel and flights had been purchased for the wedding party to Bora Bora, which was a French Polynesian Island. Layla thought that it would be too expensive and wanted to get married in a church. However Mike and his family wanted something exclusive and said that the expenses were paid by them for everything. Layla said okay and asked her pastor to travel with them to marry them.

Mike had started coming to the church regularly with Layla and her family and had given the church lots of money. Mike didn't really think that Layla knew how he was going to give her the world because he loved her so much and he couldn't put a price on how much she was worth to him. He loved the fact that she

A Scared Life to a Loving Wife

was just his pretty, young down-to-earth fiancée who didn't ask for anything and wanted to be independent. Mike thought that he couldn't wait to give her everything she wanted and desired.

20.
The Week of the Wedding

It was the Tuesday before the wedding date on Saturday, April 16th, and Layla and her family and friends were getting ready to fly out Wednesday. Mike wanted everyone to arrive early so there would be no issues or no mistakes with his and his future wife's wedding day. Layla and Mike had everything packed and a lot of her things were going to be delivered so she wouldn't have to bring so much on the plane. Her dress was big and had a long train and made her look like the angel she was. Some of the wedding guests had left already and the rest were on their way.

Mike and Layla did their last-minute packing and headed to the airport with the security team. Word had gotten around very fast and the city knew that the most eligible bachelor wouldn't be a bachelor for long. Layla and Mike were scheduled to be at their hotel room by Wednesday, and Layla planned to get up with the wedding party one more time to make sure that everyone had made it safely and knew what the plans were for all the events that were already planned for getting ready for the wedding.

On Thursday, the girls would go get nails, pedicures and massages. They would hang out and eat dinner and then on Friday the girls would get their hair done by either Felicia or Rhonda so that they would all look the same. The rehearsal dinner would be at 6 p.m. and then

A Scared Life to a Loving Wife

the girls would take Layla with them so that the groom and bride will not see each other until the wedding day on Saturday. Mike and his boys would also hang out and do their own thing and then everyone would show up early at 2 p.m., since the wedding was at 4 p.m.

Layla was super excited to have all the people she loved on one exotic island and there was so much to do. Layla's dress and other things were being delivered to her mother and sister's suite on Friday morning. Layla thought that she had everything she needed when she realized that she didn't have a ring for Mike and that she needed to write her wedding vows. Layla panicked. She decided that this would be something the girls would help her with so that she wouldn't have to shop alone. Of course Mike would send a team of security guards because he was ensuring that nothing would happen to them especially after the last event.

Everyone was starting to arrive on the Island and called her to let her know. Mike and she decided to get dinner and go to sleep early because the rest of her week would be full of excitement and she needed her beauty rest. They had a nice dinner and Mike gave Layla a hot bubble bath and told her how much he wanted and needed her and that he couldn't wait until Saturday after the wedding. Layla blushed and then got nervous thinking that Saturday night would be the very first time that they would go all the way. She didn't know what to expect, however whatever happened it would be okay because she would be Mrs. Keaton.

Mike and Layla went to their nice room and laid in the bed with Mike holding Layla. They fell fast asleep, dreaming about their futures after they were married. When Layla woke up, the sun was already shining and it was such a beautiful day outside. Layla looked over and caught a glimpse of her soon to be husband in a peaceful rest. She didn't want to wake him up. She tried to get out of bed without waking him up only to turn and see that he was smiling at her. He grabbed her and asked where she was running off to and joked with her about Layla leaving him and not wanting to be his wife. Layla assured him that she would never leave him and that she would always love him. He took her in an embrace and kissed her passionately and immediately awoke his sexual desire for her. He pulled out of it and said that he apologized and that they better start getting the day started with the wedding events.

Layla asked Mike for his ring size. Mike realized that Layla was about to buy him a ring and he let her know that he had already purchased their matching set of bands because he didn't want her to be worried. He also let her know that they also needed to make time to handle business with his CPA because he wanted her to have access to all his accounts and her own cards so that she would never have to worry about money or how to pay for anything that she wanted. Layla was amazed and asked if he was sure because she wasn't interested in his money. He told her that when you love and trust someone money doesn't mean a thing and when you get married it becomes ours and not his. Layla realized how she loved this man so much and was glad that she was about to become Mrs. Keaton.

She put on her clothes. Her friends called, trying to

A Scared Life to a Loving Wife

find out where to meet on the island for the pedicure, manicure and massage. They were all pumped and ready to see her walk down the aisle. Security was with them and the girls had a blast. Of course, there were plenty of men trying to talk with them but they politely declined and told them that they were all in relationships and about to be married.

The girls felt spoiled and they thought it was time to get something to eat. They found a nice restaurant close by and decided to sit down and talk. Layla also thought that this would be a good time to start writing her vows to her husband and she knew she was going to have to practice so that she wouldn't cry her makeup off. The girls had a lot to talk about and Mike had given Layla ample money to put in the bank to accommodate her and her friends. Layla had never had so much money in her bank account, but Mike was always trying to give her more or access to his credit card so that she would just be able to save hers. She was nervous to be added to all his accounts meaning she was going to have millions at her fingertips, which could make her a target. She would talk with Mike to make sure that she was being smart about everything.

She finished writing her vows with the girls and they were able to get her caught up on what was going on in their relationships. It looks like she would be going to two more weddings very soon because her friends had both set dates for next year. This was so exciting. All of them would be married and almost done with school, which would be another step in their lives.

Layla's phone rang and it was Mike checking to make sure the girls were enjoying themselves. He asked if they all wanted to meet the guys at the hot tub at their resorts. Layla and the girls agreed and said it would be nice just to relax. They finished up there and decided to go back to their resorts to get their bathing suits to meet them at the hot tub. They changed and met the guys down and she noticed that Mike was so sexy in his swimwear. He and his friends looked like models out of a magazine. They all were so fit. Layla thought that was why they all hooked up because they were all each other's match. They all made good couples and others looking from the outside in were jealous.

They sat down with their mates and relaxed. The water felt good and everyone was enjoying their time with each other. Mike looked at Layla and had to hold back the feelings he had for her. Her hair was so curly when it got wet and he loved to see her natural beauty.

They sat and talked as it was getting dark and decided it was time to go their separate ways to get some rest. Tomorrow was the day before the big day and they had plenty of plans for the wedding. Layla got out and dried her body and heard her phone ring. It was her mother. She was letting her know that everything arrived and that she had all the plans together for the rehearsal dinner and wanted to see her before everything got started tomorrow. She also mentioned that her sisters' dresses fit really nicely and they couldn't wait to be in the wedding. Layla let them know that she was winding down for tonight and that

A Scared Life to a Loving Wife

she would be over to their resort tomorrow to stay because that is where all the women would be Friday night. Her mother prayed for them all on the phone and told her goodnight and that she would see her tomorrow.

Mike and Layla were back in the resort about to take a shower. Mike took off his clothes and Layla did the same. She zoned right down on Mike's physique. It was mesmerizing, which made Layla a little bit excited. Layla told herself that she must wait because it is not fair to keep leading Mike on. Mike watched Layla's body and his thoughts went to erotica which he had to change before he allowed himself to be distracted from holding out. They showered and got into the bed, talked a little bit. Mike started rubbing Layla's scalp which caused her to drift off in a peaceful sleep.

Layla was awakened by a bad dream where she was being chased by one of the guys that tried to talk to her when she was with the girls. Layla laid in the bed awhile and realized that she was probably still dealing with a little post traumatic stress after all the things that had happened to her in her life. She laid there for a moment, said a prayer and drifted back into a peaceful sleep where she dreamed that she was on a shopping spree and had so many bags that she needed four men to carry them. She slept peacefully for the rest of the night.

21.
The Big Change for Everyone

Layla woke up and it was a very nice day. It was Friday, and not only a Friday but one of the most important Fridays in her life. It was the day before her wedding and the wedding events were starting today. She had a little anxiety but Layla was sure that every bride had that anxiety before their big day.

Layla wasn't out of bed well before she heard all the girls in the front room already laughing and having a good time. She got up to wash up and put on her clothes but, before that could even happen, the girls were in her room dressed with shirts that had their titles of who they were in the wedding. They gave her a shirt that said Bride and said that she would be in their hands until after the wedding.

Mike was already gone with his own boys. Everyone was to meet back together for the rehearsal dinner that would start at 6 p.m.

It was early and they were all heading over to get their hair done with Felicia and Rhonda who were also ready for her big day as well. Layla did a check to ensure that everything was in place and the girls assured her that the wedding planner was on her game and they had never seen someone so organized as she and her crew. She had everyone on point and had contacts for everyone that was needed for a wedding. Layla knew that Mike would not want it any other way,

A Scared Life to a Loving Wife

so she tried to relax. Still, this was all too much. The girls had the schedule that was given by Mike and the planners and there was a camera crew coming in to take pictures of them getting their hair done so that they would have photos for their book for later.

Layla told them that she had to stop by her mother and sister's suite because she had to get her dress, but her mother was already a step ahead of her. Her mother was in the other room hanging up her things and making sure that her daughter had everything she needed for her big day. Layla entered the room and saw her mother sitting on the bed in deep thought with tears in her eyes. Layla sat with her and held her. Her mother looked at her and admired how pretty and strong her daughter had become. She said that she would soon be Mrs. Keaton, which made her so proud. Her mom was proud that she was pure and that she held out for her husband who was God sent from above for her daughter. They sat in conversation and reminisced about when she was younger and how she had become a beautiful woman. Her mother kissed her and told her to stay on schedule because she wanted to ensure that they didn't miss anything on the agenda so that she wouldn't be stressed tomorrow. Her mother let her know that they would see her at the rehearsal dinner because she too had things that needed to be done before dinner tonight.

The girls came in and did a group hug with Layla's mother and said that they were now going to kidnap the bride until night. They got to the hairdressers' suite in time and got started on getting pretty. The camera crew was there snapping pictures doing what they were told to do, and the girls were all talking about how fun this was and how lucky Layla was to have met such a gentleman. The girls were all getting their hair like a halo braid with pin curls, which was an updo. The maid of honor was getting a slightly different style so that she could stand out just a little. Layla thought how fun it was to hang out with all the people she cared about and how good her sisters got along with her best friends. Felicia and Rhonda were very busy and there was a breakfast spread there from the maid who always cooked great food, so that everyone could eat.

Layla was in deep thought when her fiancé called to see how the plans were going. He expressed how he felt lonely without her and that he was going to be the happiest man in the world after tomorrow. Layla blushed and told him that he had done a great job with making sure everyone and everything was in place for their big day. Layla let him know that she would miss him tonight and couldn't wait for him to hold her tomorrow. He reminded her that she had no reason to be worried about anything, that his parents had put the finishing touches on everything and made sure everything was in place and that she was going to be the most beautiful bride in the world. Layla blushed and realized how much she loved this man. He said that he would let her get back to the girls and he was getting back with the boys who were talking about how pretty her friends were going to be tomorrow. They were so in love with her friends as well.

They both said their goodbyes as Layla was called

A Scared Life to a Loving Wife

to get into the chair to start her hair. She was going to let Felicia hook her up because she had no idea how she would need her hair. Hours seemed to go by when the girls said that everyone was staying in the bride's suite which was not too far from the hairdressers and Beauty and the Beatz. The makeup artist was scheduled at 3 p.m., so everyone needed to be in place and at the wedding site by 2 p.m. It was about 4 p.m. and the rehearsal dinner started at 6 p.m. Layla's hair was up in pins, so that it would be easy to finish tomorrow on her big day.

Layla was beginning to get a little tired. The girls went back to gather all their things to take them to Layla's suite and make themselves comfortable. They made sure they got all their stuff and headed to the suite. When they got to the suite they noticed the door was already open and Layla's mother and sisters were there getting everything ready for them. Layla tied her hair in the bonnet and laid across the couch for a little while to catch a little nap before the rehearsal and the girls joined her and continued to talk, eat snacks and relax. Layla got a little shut eye and, before you knew it, she had to get up and start getting ready for the rehearsal dinner.

It was being held in a huge ballroom overlooking the water and the resort. The view was absolutely gorgeous. The wedding planner was doing her thing making sure everyone was doing their job to make this occasion flawless. When the wedding party came in, she stopped and came to greet all of them. She told Layla how gorgeous she was and how she was going to be the highlight of the occasion. She immediately started to get people in line for the big day and talked with them about how things would be flowing tomorrow.

There were cameras everywhere snapping pictures and when Mike and his parents came in camera crews were trying to get the pictures. It was definitely a celebrity occasion and Layla was starting to get nervous. Tonya saw her sister's anxiety and went to comfort her and let her know that everything was going to be okay and that she would be here with her the entire time. Layla felt much better, and then in walked Mike and his friends who looked as if they stepped out of a GQ magazine. They had on linen suits with expensive shoes and when they walked in everyone looked their way. The people who were setting up the dinner looked to see all the fine men walking into the room and knew that they were important. Mike was looking for one woman only which made the others jealous.

Mike's friends found who they were looking for and everyone started to practice what was supposed to happen except for the bride and groom. Someone walked to show them their part for the big day. Layla's mother knew that she would have to light the unity candle along with Mike's parents. The DJ was very comfortable with his part and how the wedding would flow with the help of the wedding planner. The decorators were doing an amazing job and the place was already looking really nice. The decorating team said that they were not near complete.

A Scared Life to a Loving Wife

Time was going by really fast and, after practicing a couple of times, the wedding party had it down to the tee. The DJ knew what songs to play and when to play them and everyone knew their cue of when to walk down the aisle.

Mike watched Layla in awe and knew that she was going to take his breath away tomorrow. She was already beautiful, even though she had pins in her hair. His imagination went to after the wedding night and the things he would do to her and how he could finally get her whole body. He was in deep thought when he was interrupted that it was time to go eat.

There were all kinds of food to eat, served buffet style and the food was so good. The caterers did an amazing job so she knew the food would be on point tomorrow. Everyone sat down and ate and spoke to one another like everyone was already family. Mike's parents really loved Layla's mother. They could talk for hours. The DJ played some music so people started having a good time.

It was getting a little late and Mike and the boys and Layla and the girls went their separate ways to enjoy the last night that she would be single. The girls decided to take Layla out to a club they saw when they were getting manicures and pedicures earlier because it had karaoke and good food. The girls also said that there would be a DJ at night, so it seemed like the place to hang out for some good, clean fun.

They got to the club about 10:30 and it was already packed. They got a private table and sat down enjoying the scenery. She and her crew had attracted a lot of eyes from men and women. Patrons knew they were somebody special because they had their own personal security. People had recognized her from when she had been on television with the most eligible bachelor and they were definitely jealous. There were men who wanted to be in their crew but, after seeing how big her ring was, they had to think and blink twice.

Security was very strict about not letting anyone get into their circle and Layla understood why after what had already happened before. There were others that had seen her on the news from what happened to her and felt sorry for her and said how lucky she was to still be alive. The girls let them know that this was her night before her wedding, so they wanted nothing but good vibes. They understood and told her congratulations. They expressed how lucky she was to be marrying Michael Keaton. Layla knew that she would eventually have to get used to paparazzi and admirers so she better start now.

The DJ played one of her favorite songs so she and her friends went to dance on the dance floor and the men were all up in there faces. The security would not let them even get close enough to touch so they could only watch. Layla and her friends were killing them and afterwards they went into a private room in the back for a surprise. Layla didn't know what the girls were up to but when she got back there it was like a private area where they put a blindfold on her and sat her in a comfortable chair. It seemed like forever and finally she heard some slow music playing. They took the blindfold off and a fine stripper was right in her

A Scared Life to a Loving Wife

face dancing in her area. Layla was so embarrassed that her friends had hired a stripper to dance for them. He was good looking, strong and was able to move his hips like your imagination. The girls gave him tips and then he picked her up and danced with her as if they were a couple. Layla suddenly didn't feel right with God because of the atmosphere and because this man wasn't her husband. He whispered in her ear what and how he could make her feel after the party and Layla asked if he would put her down. She tipped him and he went over to dance with her friends. Layla felt very uncomfortable in that environment. She made a mental note that this would be the last time she would come into a club because it seemed that men didn't have any respect when you're already involved with someone.

Layla started to think about what would happen tomorrow night with her husband, which put fear in her heart that she wouldn't be able to satisfy him. The girls felt the mood change and paid the stripper and went over to see what was wrong with their bride. She told them that she was a little nervous about tomorrow night because she was still a virgin and they had been waiting a long time. The girls assured her that everything would be fine and that they were getting ready to go back to the resort. The security cleared the path and they left to go back to the suite where everyone was making sure they had everything they needed before the big day.

Layla thanked her friends for taking her out and said that she was going to relax in the jacuzzi tub for a while. The girls said that would be a good idea and everyone started to find places to sleep which wasn't that hard because the suite had plenty of beds. Layla relaxed in the tub and then laid down on the bed to get some sleep. She knew that it was going to be a big day tomorrow and she was going to need plenty of rest. Layla drifted off to sleep and slept peacefully all night long with her friends close by her.

22.
The Wedding Day

Layla woke up and laid in the bed just thinking how this day was really about to happen. She reflected back on the very first day that she had met Mike and how she thought about him daily after meeting him. She also reflected back on how he not only saved her but her mother and her sisters and now everyone was living a better life and had met new people as well.

Layla was snapped out of her thoughts by the girls coming in and letting her know that it was time to start getting gorgeous for her amazing day. She knew that she had a lot to do but she knew that she would have to start the day off with breakfast just in case she was too excited to eat anything else. Layla told her friends to contact the maid so that she could do her magic and asked what time the hairdressers and Beauty and the Beatz would be coming. The girls said that they would be at the suite around 11 a.m. along with the camera crew that was in charge of taking pictures while she was getting dressed to be able to capture the before and after photos of the wedding.

Layla was excited and nervous at the same time. This would be the night that her husband and her would be able to go all the way, whatever that meant. Layla got up and went to wash up before breakfast and to put on something very comfortable.

She wasn't in the bathroom long when she heard

her sisters and mom talking to the girls asking where their baby and bride to be was at? Her mother and sisters opened the bathroom door and joined her while she was taking her bath and shaving. Layla and her family were so close and her mother and sisters were very excited for her. Her mother was letting her know that she didn't have anything to worry about because she had already prayed and knew Mike was the one for her. They all prayed while she was in the bathroom and then her mother and sisters left to get all her things prepared for her to be a bride.

On the other hand, Mike was very excited. He didn't sleep all night because he couldn't wait for this moment where Layla would be all his. He imagined what she would look like when she was coming down the aisle and he couldn't wait to share his vows with her because they were from his heart. His boys had taken him out the night before, but all Mike could think about was his soon to be wife and no other girl or woman mattered at all. Mike felt that the time was going in slow motion and he couldn't wait until 4 p.m.

His mother and father expressed how happy they were to him and how Layla and her family were great people to be added to their family. His mother was worried about what Layla would do in front of the camera, but Mike assured her that it didn't matter as long as he was able to have his bride.

The guest list was about 300, which was a lot of people who wanted to be in attendance of a wedding thrown by one of the richest families there was. However security was tight and everyone had to go

A Scared Life to a Loving Wife

through screening before entering the wedding.

Mike couldn't afford any mistakes in making this day not perfect for his bride. He knew he would love her for as long as he lived and she was the only thing that mattered to him. Mike was too excited to eat anything but his mother June made sure that he at least ate a little because with all the excitement he may not be able to eat again until after the ceremony.

The wedding planners had everything in place and the resort had been booked fully for the event, meaning that everyone there was either part of the wedding party or a guest of the wedding party. The time was getting a little late, so Mike called his friends to see what their status was and to assure everything was in place and that, of course, the guys had everything they needed to make their day special.

Back at the ladies' suite, the girls were really getting beautiful. The hairdressers were touching up the girls' hairstyles to ensure that no piece was out of place. Layla's hair was being pinned up and looking like a barbie doll. Felicia was doing some pin curls in her hair on the side into a ball along with a twisted up halo around her head making her look like the angel that Mike saw her to be. To make her hair even better, Felicia put real diamond jewelry in her hair to put the finishing touches on her hair. All the girls were taking their own pictures of her and holding back tears because of how beautiful Layla was. She didn't even have on makeup and she was already drop dead gorgeous. The camera crew was even amazed at how beautiful she was and they could see why the eligible rich bachelor wanted her so much. When her hair was done, they put on her other jewelry which made it all come to life.

The makeup artist was doing an amazing job on the girls and, when she looked to see how beautiful her sisters were, Layla had to hold back her own tears. Seeing everyone so pretty was a lot on her and she was glad that she didn't have her makeup on yet so she could get her cries out now and not have to start the process over again. The girls started to put on their dresses so that they could help Layla get hers on. The girls' dresses were lavender and the maid of honor's dress was slightly different than the rest. Layla admired how good her wedding party looked and they were really going to look good on camera.

Layla's dress was very big and the train was very long. She decided to get her makeup done first before putting on the dress since it was one that she could step into. Her makeup was done naturally because her face was already gorgeous without it. The artist reminded her that she wanted to show her natural beauty because that is what her husband was attracted to already. Layla agreed and did as little as possible. She did a little foundation, lashes, eye shadow and of course the lips had to pop. Layla looked like a famous model who was going to a concert.

Layla and her friends started to put on her dress because time was nearing close and she decided to just put on the main part of the dress and the heels and bring the train to be put on at the wedding spot room. Her dress fit just right. It was tight fitting in the top because

A Scared Life to a Loving Wife

she had the body for it and the bottom flared out and the train was long. The girls watched the makeup artist and the hairdresser dress her, holding back tears to avoid messing up their makeup. Layla's mother was already wiping tears and her sisters were trying not to cry. Layla looked in the mirror and wondered who this new woman was standing in front of her. She was amazed at how pretty she was. Layla went to the room to grab her heels, flats, her vows and her garter belt so that she would have it all at the wedding site. She put it in her bag and grabbed her formal purse that went with her wedding dress.

The girls were doing the same thing because the stretched limos were already parked out front with nice drivers and security waiting for the bride and her party to get in the car. The guys were gentlemen who helped all the women in the cars and made sure the bride was in safely. The security had strict directions on assuring that all the people arrived safely. The limos headed towards the wedding spot and Layla was really thinking that this was really about to happen. When they arrived at the wedding spot, the camera crew and news crews were already there trying to catch everyone when entering the wedding spot.

There were limos already present meaning the guys and the groom were already there and had their camera time so that the groom and bride wouldn't see each other. When the limos stopped camera crews were already running to the car because they knew the bride had arrived. Layla felt nervous but the security was on it. Layla smiled for the camera but didn't answer any questions. The girls and she walked in where the wedding planners were directing them on where they should go until time comes. It was still about forty-five minutes before the wedding started, so they had time to put the finishing touches on her beauty. Layla and her crew got to the room and were told by the wedding planners that they had just a little time and that the groomsmen were already seating the guests and that the pastor was already in place. She said that she would be back in a little while to start lining them up in their spots just like they had practiced at the rehearsal dinner.

Layla didn't know that weddings could be so stressful. She could feel an anxiety attack trying to creep up. Tonya noticed that Layla was looking a little flustered, so she came to the rescue. She made Layla sit down and got her some water and helped her with her breathing techniques. She understood that this was a lot on her younger sister and she wouldn't let her have to face it alone.

The hairdresser and Beauty and the Beatz were checking to make sure that all the girls were looking their best. Then they focused on Layla's hair and makeup and asked if it would be okay if they would help her with her accessories and her train. Layla snapped back into reality and grabbed her bag so that she could be ready. She slid her blue garter belt up around her thigh and put her perfume on her body and her dress. The girls helped snap her train onto her dress which really made her look like an angel from heaven, lost on earth. Everyone admired how beautiful she was

A Scared Life to a Loving Wife

and the time was getting near.

There was a knock on the door, followed by an opening of the door with the wedding crew coming in to take the ladies to their spot except for the maid of honor. She was instructed to follow the bride who would be going through another way to dodge all the other guests so she would be in the room by the aisle. Layla heard the song letting her know that the wedding had started with the walking of the parents which means that it wouldn't be long before she would be walking down the aisle to become Mrs. Keaton. There were pictures being taken of her before walking down the aisle where Layla was able to give a smile and look her best. Layla heard the song change which meant the bridesmaids and the maid of honor would be next to get in place. Layla knew that it was show time because she would then walk after the flower girls on the runway.

Layla was thinking that she hoped that she didn't forget to do anything when the wedding planner tapped her and asked if she was ready. She shook her head yes and the doors opened and everyone was standing. The song played by Major, "This Is Why I Love You" played loud. The altar seemed like a long walk especially while all eyes were on her. She grabbed Mike's father's arm and they walked hand in hand down the aisle. She heard everyone sniffling and saying how beautiful she was. She looked up and saw angels hanging in the ceiling and the scene looked like heaven on earth. The news crews and the photographers were snapping pictures away and she also felt someone straightening out her long train. When she got close enough she could see Mike in tears of excitement and the wedding party was also in tears. Layla's mother was smiling in tears and Layla felt her mother's strength so that she could make it through.

When Layla reached the front the music faded and everyone was told to take a seat. The preacher asked, "Who gives this lady to this man," and Layla's mother and Mike's father said that they will. The ceremony went as planned and Layla and Mike had everyone in tears with the vows that they wrote for each other.

When doing the ring exchange Layla was so amazed that Mike had the biggest and most beautiful diamond she had ever seen. She thought about how this ring would weigh her finger down and everyone in the back could see that Mike meant business when he picked it. Mike had bought him a match with the band, which looked really good as a set.

The ceremony ended as the Pastor said, "You may kiss your bride," and Mike kissed her for it seemed like eternity. Then it was time to turn to the front of the church and the pastor pronounced them husband and wife and introduced them as Mr. and Mrs. Keaton.

Everyone stood and congratulated them and they walked out of the church followed by the wedding party. They were led to a ballroom for snacks and drinks to mix and mingle until photos were taken. The reception was very nice and the DJ did his part by introducing the wedding party, doing the dances with the parents and their first dance. Mike stared into Layla's eyes during the dance and Layla could feel his

A Scared Life to a Loving Wife

excitement in his pants already. They were so in love with each other and enjoying this day to the fullest. The food was amazing, the cake scene was fun.

Mike acted a fool when it was time to remove the garter belt. Layla noticed when Mike threw the garter belt that there were men actually trying to catch it instead of running from it. Mike's friend, who was one of the ones dating Layla's friend, caught the belt. When it was time to throw the bouquet all the single ladies were fighting to get it. Layla tossed it up and Lina caught it. She was a match to Mike's friend who caught the garter belt. They kissed and took pictures and everyone was excited.

The rest of the night went smoothly. Everyone danced, celebrated and congratulated the new couple. There were plenty of gifts and cards from the guests and they were going to need lots of help carrying it all back. Time was passing and guests started to leave. Mike and Layla decided that it was time to spend time together so they started saying their goodnights to their parents and their friends. The security saw that the bride and groom started to go towards the limo and the driver was ready to work. The driver congratulated them and took them to their wedding night suite which was different from where they were getting ready for the wedding. When they pulled up it was at a different part of the island and it was beautiful. The weather was perfect and while Layla was in thought she didn't see that Mike had picked her up and was carrying her to their suite. She smiled and trusted that her husband would keep her safe.

23.
First Time for Everything

Mike and Layla entered their suite and it was nothing but beautiful. It was decorated for the bride and groom. It had Welch's sparkling grape juice, wine glasses and everything they needed to set the mood. Mike lit candles, turned on some music and stared at Layla with those seductive eyes. Layla looked back at him with her innocent bedroom eyes.

He told his Mrs. Keaton to come dance with him and she complied. She seductively gave him a show and teased him until she could feel his manhood rise to the challenge. He kissed her on her neck and on her lips and the mood was definitely shifting faster than Layla expected. They were letting moans escape from their lips. Mike started to help Layla out of her dress while Layla was helping Mike out of his tuxedo.

This would be the first time they would go all the way, the first time Layla would give her virginity away. Layla's heart was beating faster trying to anticipate what this moment was going to be like. The kisses got more passionate and the mood was shifting again. Mike felt he had waited all his life to be able to finally share this moment with the woman he loved from the moment he saw her in the grocery store.

He carried her to the bed and laid her down. He planted soft kisses on her neck and her entire body not wanting to miss a single spot. He enjoyed listening to

A Scared Life to a Loving Wife

the music they were making together and he didn't want it to stop. He continued to follow the music while he made love to his wife for the very first time. It was all that he imagined and it felt much better that they were married so this was ordained by the Lord above. The mood seemed to last for a while and Layla's eyes were telling Mike that she was enjoying the love making and that she was nervous but comfortable at the same time.

After they were done, they decided to take a bubble bath together in the jacuzzi so that they could relax and come down off the high that they were both on. Mike ensured that Layla was okay and she said that she felt good now that it had happened for the first time. Layla wanted to make sure that she had satisfied her husband and got confirmation when Mike told her that she was all he would ever need and that he would never stop loving and making love to her. She smiled and they went to relax in the bathtub. The jacuzzi was very relaxing and both of them had such a long day that they were both nodding off in each other's arms. They got out of the tub and laid in each other's arms for what seemed like eternity. Layla felt that she was the luckiest woman in the world and she fell fast asleep in her husband's big arms while he sheltered her from any fears that she had.

Layla was sleeping so peacefully when she was woken up by sunlight in the room windows. They slept until the next morning. When she rolled over, Mike was staring into her eyes and his manhood seemed to be ready again. Layla followed its lead and got on top of him to give him what he wanted. Layla felt empowered that she was able to take the lead and satisfy her husband. She went to clean herself up and went into the kitchen to find them something to eat. When she got in the kitchen, she noticed that there wasn't much in the refrigerator. She made a call to the maids to tell them what she and her husband wanted to eat.

Most of the wedding party was leaving to go back to the states today so she wanted to see them off so that she could continue to enjoy her honeymoon with her husband. She called her friends and they wanted to know how the night went. She let them know that it was amazing and that she wasn't scared anymore. They let her know that they would get with her when she returned and that they were getting ready to ride the plane home with their boyfriends, who were already into her best friends like Mike was into Layla.

Layla sat back and thought how one man and his family helped change not only her life but her entire family's lives as well. She told them that she loved them and to call when they landed. They promised that they would.

Layla called her mother and sisters, whose plane was not leaving until later. They were having so much fun with Mike's parents that they were not thinking about her. Layla was glad to see her mother and sisters so happy and couldn't wait to be able to put her and her sisters in a nice, gated home of their choice, with a security team to protect them at all times. Mike had already talked to her and let her know that her family

A Scared Life to a Loving Wife

would always be safe with him.

Mike must have noticed Layla in deep thought because he asked to pay her for her thoughts. She smiled and told him that she was just thinking on how blessed she was to be Mrs. Keaton. Mike told her that he would always take care of her and her family, that she had nothing to worry about. Mike told her that he had lots of plans for her while they were on their honeymoon and that they would have plenty of time to talk business. Layla agreed and told her husband to take the lead and Mike told her that it was his pleasure to do so.

24.
Two Months Later......

Layla still felt tired from the honeymoon, but she knew she had to get back to the everyday hustle and bustle. She got caught up at school because this was her senior year and it wasn't no joke. Layla took her final exams, aced them and was preparing to graduate this year. Her plan was to enroll for her Masters and achieve her doctoral degree in Psychology. Her friends and she had plans and they all were going to finish them as they promised.

Layla noticed that she had been very nauseated lately and couldn't eat certain things without feeling that she wanted to be sick. She had been so busy being a bride, student and everything else that she didn't even realize that she was late with her cycle. She started to panic but calmed down when she realized that she was married now and she could just talk to her husband.

Mike was talking to his lawyer and accountant about how, now that everything was legal, he wanted to add his wife to his accounts and include her in every decision that was made. Mike was always fair and wanted to make sure that he upheld his part in being the best husband that he could be to his queen.

He noticed that Layla was looking a little nervous, so he called her to come sit on his lap. She came over and it seemed that she looked more beautiful everyday. Her hair had gotten longer and her skin was flawless

A Scared Life to a Loving Wife

but he had noticed that she had picked up a little weight. She looked thicker than she was when he met her. She was just drop dead gorgeous every time he saw her. He asked her if she was okay and she told him that she was a little overwhelmed about school and graduation and that she felt that she might have a stomach bug or something.

Mike had the maid bring her some ginger ale and that she should try to get a little rest. She then told him that she thought that the stress could have caused her to be late with her menstrual cycle. Mike looked into her eyes with the happiest look on his face like he just hit the jackpot. He asked her if she thought she could be pregnant. Layla looked and nervousness took hold of the mood and Mike came in to save it, saying, "Baby, I would be the happiest man in the world. We should take a home pregnancy test."

Layla agreed and Mike had the maid pick up two of the best ones. Mike grabbed Layla into a bear hug and couldn't wait to see the test results. The maid came back with the tests and Mike and Layla read the directions so that they wouldn't mess them up. Layla and Mike went into the bathroom, took the test and waited for the results. Immediately two lines appeared indicating that Layla was with child.

Mike was so happy and Layla was so nervous. She wanted to be a mom, but she didn't know that it would come so soon. She knew that the media was about to have a field day and it probably wouldn't stop. Mike and Layla decided to make a doctor's appointment for the next day as well to confirm what Layla already knew because she was definitely feeling very sick. Mike was already on the phone with his mother and father who were very excited that they were about to be grandparents. His mother was already trying to move them back closer so that she could help with the baby. Layla told her family and they were happy as well.

Everyone seemed happier than Layla who was already struggling with pregnancy and realized that it probably would get worse. She went to rest a little because the nausea was something serious. Layla didn't get sick much at all before this pregnancy.

Layla woke up dry heaving and throwing up and Mike ran into defense mode helping her. He was right by her side, holding her hair and offering a wet towel and water. Mike wanted the baby but he didn't want Layla to be feeling bad, so he would mention getting her something to help her with her nausea from the doctor.

Mike assured Layla she would get the best care after the doctor confirmed the results and gave her about how many weeks she was. The doctor confirmed that Layla was around 10 weeks pregnant. He talked to them about the importance of the first trimester and that the morning sickness would get better. The doctor prescribed some nausea medicine, prenatal vitamins and plenty of rest.

Mike assured the doctor he would take care of her and that he was very excited. Layla's mom and sisters came to stay at the mansion with them because Mike didn't want her home alone while he had to do business.

A Scared Life to a Loving Wife

The media was hounding Layla because they got word of the pregnancy. The world was excited for the new life that Mike was living. Layla laid in her mother's lap and her mother told her that when she was pregnant with her she was very sick and it could be possible that it could be a girl. Layla thought about how their baby would look just like Mike, handsome, strong and beautiful. She was glad that she waited for her husband to bring a baby into this world. She realized that lately in her life she had done a lot of things for the first time and now she was about to be a first time mother to her husband's child.

25.
The End Has Come

Layla was finally getting the hang of carrying a child. Mike was always talking to the baby or touching and holding her all the time. Pregnancy really looked good on Layla. She was perfect. The weight was in the right places and she had the perfect basketball shaped belly. Layla was 12 weeks and the sonogram revealed that they were having a healthy baby girl. Mike was so happy and he just imagined that the baby would look identical to his queen. Layla's appetite had picked up and the sickness was getting much better. Both families were so excited and they all wanted to start making a nursery and planning a shower.

Layla sat eating a snack on the couch with her husband when the news started talking about her case with her stalker. Layla and Mike zoomed in as the news recapped what happened earlier, saying that the judge had sentenced Wilson to life in prison with no parole. He would have gotten the death penalty, however he died the previous night in prison and his death was being investigated.

Layla's eyes were glued to that television and her mouth was wide open. What happened? Layla didn't even have time to confront him face to face, to tell him that she wasn't scared anymore. Layla closed her eyes and said a silent prayer that God would forgive her and that he had time to make it right with God before

A Scared Life to a Loving Wife

leaving this earth. Layla started to feel sorry for him knowing that he was also a victim. She even started to cry for him.

Mike realized and grabbed her, knowing that his wife loved everyone even if they did wrong. She felt relieved and sad at the same time. It may have been her hormones out of control but at the moment she noticed that this is why she chose psychology and that she would see her own therapist to continue to cope with the life that she was dealt. She was glad that God had mercy on her life and blessed her beyond what she asked him for and gave her a man who loved God first.

Layla and Mike didn't miss a church service and vowed to always put God first and each other next. They were blessed, favored by God and wanted to make sure that their children would always put God first. Layla and Mike had all they could ever want or have and had two great families who worked well together and were about to have a beautiful daughter to love and adore. Layla walked across the stage with confidence to receive her bachelor's degree in psychology and watched her friends walk as well with their degrees. Everyone was able to see her dreams come true.

Mike and Layla decided to let her mom and sisters stay in the mansion together with them so that Layla would have enough help with the baby. Mike and Layla also bought a mansion in New York so that they would be able to come home to his parents' house so that they could also be involved with the baby. Life was good and nobody would have known that a little project girl who had a not so good life could still be blessed and favored by God to have everything she ever wanted and dreamed to have. Who would have known that Layla's scary life would make her into a loving wife?

The End

Inspirations

First, I want to give Honor to my Lord and Savior Jesus Christ who gave me grace and mercy to stand through bad times. I want to thank my husband, my family, my best friends, my fans and my publisher Mike Simpson for believing in me to write my first book. I wanted to write this book to bring awareness to stalking and that stalkers are really real. If you are in this situation, please do your part in getting the authorities involved as much as possible. Statistics show that this happens more than it is talked about and the women don't end up as lucky as I was. Women, always watch your surroundings and never ever lead a man on if you are not interested in him. If you have a partner on your team, never withhold information from them so that they can also help you stay safe. My book is inspired by some real life events that happen every day. Thank you so much to everyone who has purchased and read my book and I truly hope that you enjoyed it.

About The Author

My name is Tamelia Keaton known as Mia. I was born in Winston-Salem, NC and have been residing here all my life. I am married to Miguel Keaton who is a disabled veteran. Together we have five sons and one bonus son. I am a person who loves traveling to see different places with my family, Zumba with my zumba family, hanging out with my church family and writing in my spare time. I went to Carver High School where I obtained my diploma and enjoyed running track. I obtained my Bachelor's degree graduating Cum Laude in Healthcare Management with a specialization in Gerontology from American Intercontinental University in Atlanta Georgia and pledging to be a part of Alpha Sigma Lambda, the Honors Society club as well. I have had a long career with Food Lion having the pleasure of being a Customer Service Manager and managing a frontend. I have also had the honors of working for Wells Fargo Bank where I experienced every role in retail and having the pleasure to becoming a Branch Manager at one of the locations in Winston. I now enjoy caregiving with private clients and supporting my own family. I enjoy motivating others to bring out their boldness and discovering their purpose for the body of Christ. I am a person who loves to serve wherever my skills are needed. I enjoy empowering women by writing books on everyday struggles and how God can turn them into testimonies.

Please look out for *Rips, Tips and Scripts*, my new book coming very soon. You cannot miss out on reading it.

Made in the USA
Middletown, DE
03 June 2025